D1249225

No Safe Place

H. L. Wegley

Romantic Suspense

Cover Design: Samantha Fury
http://www.furycoverdesign.com/

Back Cover Design: Trinity Press International
http://trinitywebworks.com/

Interior Formatting: Trinity Press International
http://trinitywebworks.com/

ISBN-13: 978-0996493772
ISBN-10: 0996493778

Also available in eBook publication

OTHER BOOKS BY H. L. WEGLEY

Against All Enemies Series
1 Voice in the Wilderness
2 Voice of Freedom
3 Chasing Freedom

Pure Genius Series
1 Hide and Seek
2 On the Pineapple Express
3 Moon over Maalaea Bay
4 Triple Threat

Witness Protection Series
1 No Safe Place
2 No True Justice – coming soon

DEDICATION

This book is dedicated to all the Jesus followers who have wandered away to the far country, or perhaps to a country not so far away, but one where they had no business going. This is the story of a man not so different from you. My hope is that you will learn from him, from his tragedies and his triumphs. As long as you have life and breath, never forget that there is a way back, a way home. You have a Heavenly Father—no, you have Abba, a Daddy, who will run with arms open to meet his returning child. What did Jesus leave undone that is needed to forgive you and remove the guilt of your prodigal life? Nothing. He did it all. Just come home.

I also dedicate this book to those who have been disowned because of their decision to follow Jesus. This is a story of a young woman whose heart is broken by such rejection. I hope you will learn from her example. The sting of rejection by family and friends can seem to eclipse the joy of your salvation. Don't let it. You have a Savior who is not willing that any should perish, so pray for your loved ones. Answer their questions, humbly. Don't try to win arguments or debates with them. But, instead, be ready to give them solid reasons for the hope you have. As long as they have life and breath, there is hope for them. May your prayers sic the relentless Hound of Heaven on them. He can pursue a heart in ways we cannot even comprehend.

CONTENTS

ACKNOWLEDGMENTS

Many thanks to Christina Tarabochia, award-winning author, editor and co-owner of Ashberry Lane Publishing, who read the original manuscript and provided advice on how to write from a woman's POV.

Thanks to my wife, Babe, for listening to me read to her all five major revisions of the story and for helping me fill the plot holes and fix the logic. Thanks to my sister-in-law Duke Gibson for reading and evaluating the story and to my critique group, Dawn Lily and Gayla Hiss, for their suggestions.

Thanks to Shahid Shafiq for the original photo used for Randi and to Derrick Cooper for the original forest scene photo.

Thank you, Samantha Fury, for creating a beautiful, wrap-around cover that captures the feel of *No Safe Place*.

Thanks to our Lord for leaving me enough wits and words to write another novel. May He bless and encourage us all through the lessons learned by Matt, a young man returning from the far country, and Randi, a young woman who was abandoned by her family because of her faith.

Let the wicked forsake his way, and the unrighteous man his thoughts: and let him return unto the Lord, and he will have mercy upon him; and to our God, for he will abundantly pardon.
Isaiah 55:7 (KJV)

Chapter 1

Olympic National Park, near La Push, Washington

They hadn't gunned him down two months ago, but it wasn't for lack of trying. The odds were Matt Mathison should have ended up planted in the ground or as a pile of bones picked clean by scavengers in the forest.

Was he lucky to have escaped? It felt more like punishment for his transgressions. Regardless, his present unity of body and soul was not a blessing. Of that, he was certain.

Matt refocused on the winding dirt trail wrinkled with tree roots along each side—roots waiting to grab the foot of a tired or careless runner. He kicked his pace up a notch as he loped along the trail traversing the ridge above the beach at La Push.

He maintained this fast but comfortable pace as he ran through towering Sitka spruce trees. Matt inhaled deep breaths of fresh, ocean-scented air.

Countless shafts of sunlight probed the shadows through openings in the forest canopy. As he ran, the myriad sunbeams created a mesmerizing, strobe-light effect on his arms.

Running in this tranquil setting helped. It helped Matt ignore that he was bone tired, emotionally drained, and spiritually in limbo. But didn't he deserve all the misery life had dealt him? All of it and a lot more.

A half mile from the parking area, the pounding of a runner's powerful feet sounded on the ridge behind him. Someone had rapidly closed on him, someone running at an incredible rate.

There were *never* other runners on this trail. Only one conclusion made sense. After two months of searching, Arellano's assassins had found him.

This remote location was supposed to give Matt several months of safety, maybe enough time to deal with his problems and get his life back on track. Why today? He hadn't even brought a gun with him.

With the cartel's powerful weapons, they could gun him down, dispose of his body here in the forest, and let the animals clean up the evidence.

The sprinting runner drew close, obviously trying to catch him. Matt had only one weapon—surprise. Surprise like the crushing, blindside tackle that sent him to the hospital for multiple surgeries. Maybe he could pass that experience on to the dude who was chasing him.

Matt dashed toward a big spruce on the inside of a sharp dogleg in the trail and slipped out of sight behind it, his heart pounding louder than the runner's footsteps.

The sound of heavy breathing came from only a few yards away.

Matt crouched, arms ready to make a perfect, bone-crushing tackle. As his coach used to say, even quarterbacks must learn to tackle to prevent their mistakes from becoming disasters.

He braced himself and shot a short prayer heavenward, doubting that it rose above the forest canopy. He tensed and focused on a section of trail beside the spruce tree.

A white Nike hit the ground in front of him.

Matt lunged forward.

* * *

Randi Richards slowed and cut to the inside of the trail. She broke stride as she hopped around a patch of mud left from the winter rain. According to the Climate Prediction Center, the strong El Nino could bring the worst drought in a hundred years to the Olympic Peninsula.

When she swerved between the mud and the large spruce tree, a blur of tanned flesh and purple flew at her from the right side.

The purple battering ram hit her thighs.

It ripped Randi's legs from under her.

Her neck whipped to one side.

As quickly as he came, her assailant broke contact, dumping her on her rear.

What just happened? An attack? She shook off her dazed confusion and prepared to fight back.

A weapon. The edge of the mud hole held a potato-sized rock. She grabbed it, cocked her throwing arm, and looked up at her target.

Two huge palms pushed toward her, hiding the face behind them. "I'm sorry. I won't hurt you. You're safe." The voice barking out those words could have belonged to a battlefield commander, except for the way it softened on the last two words.

She relaxed her arm but glared up. If only she could read his eyes. "Put your hands down."

He dropped his arms.

From her seat in the muck, she studied him. Tall, muscular, and intimidating. But those brilliant blue eyes held only sadness. Maybe sadness tinged with surprise. He had a deep tan, dark hair, and a perfectly sculpted face. His description in a single word, magnificent.

No. Infuriating!

This man had knocked her on her rear in a three-inch-deep quagmire, and now he stared at her, looking like he might actually smile about it.

"I'm so sorry, Miss, uh ... Ma'am."

"Why did you—you could've killed me! You—"

"I was trying to say I'm sorry that—"

"Sorry that you what?" She tossed the rock off the trail. "What were you trying to do and why? I deserve an explanation, don't you think?"

"Are you okay?"

He had avoided her question. "Do I look okay? I'm sitting on my fanny in a pig sty." There was a faint discoloration on her upper leg. Had it been there before? "There's a big bruise on my thigh and—" No injuries. He hadn't made the tiny bruise, and apparently there was no imminent danger.

Sprawled out in the mud she couldn't hold a lady-like pose. At least she wasn't being videoed. If her friends on the track team could only see her now.

A small giggle escaped her mouth, but this ridiculous scene deserved more than a giggle. Randi threw her head back and, for the first time in weeks, laughed.

* * *

Matt had put the brakes on his picture-perfect tackle as soon as two sleek, muscular legs and a bouncing ponytail appeared. The impact of hitting those powerful legs had wrenched his shoulder. At least he hadn't driven through her. Had he done that, something would have broken. From the looks of her legs, probably some part of him.

Now she sat in a five-point resting position on her rear, hands and feet in deep mud, staring up at him with ... those eyes, a deep, dazzling hazel. Her auburn hair blazed with fire where the sun lit it. She looked athletic and alive, thank goodness, and completely captivating. Even her anger added to her stunning looks.

Was she really alright? When he took a step toward her, her expression changed.

Belly-shaking laughter jounced her body, and her hazel eyes and ponytail danced in time with the melodious sounds.

So she wasn't hurt. And she was an athlete. A trim, fit, absolutely beautiful athlete. If she could look this good sitting in the mud, in maroon and white running shorts and a T-shirt, what might she look in a little black dress? He looked again at her auburn hair. Or maybe a green dress?

Matt, you've got to be crazy. Help her up, then you

need to disappear ... for her sake.

"Don't you think it's about time to get up out of that muddy ooze?" He tried to smile as he stretched out a hand.

"You mean like our progenitors, evolving out of that primordial ooze to stand erect?"

That expression on her face—serious or facetious? "I don't believe that nonsense."

"Good." Her grin turned to a smile, highlighting a light sprinkling of freckles across her nose. "Neither do I."

Her freckles added to his first impression of her—unpretentious, unaware of her extraordinary beauty. And he still didn't know her name.

"I'm Matt Mathison." He pushed his hand a little farther.

She pulled hers out of the quagmire and shoved a mud-caked hand at him, keeping her eyes focused on his. "I'm Randi Richards."

He studied her hand. It looked like his baby sister's after she'd been making mud pies. Wasn't she going to wipe it off first?

She kept reaching for him, smiling as mud dripped from her hand.

So, he had to shake her muddy hand. She was evening the score. Matt shook it, added his other hand, and grasped her wrist above the mud line. He pulled hard.

She broke free from the mud.

He pulled again and brought her to her feet.

She was tall, about five-foot-ten. A slender but shapely figure that was impossible to ignore. And well-developed legs. Those legs could run at the furious pace that overtook him.

He scanned upward, in no hurry to get to her face. When he did, her smile was gone.

"Are you through with your inventory?" Her eyes flashed like laser beams, while her sunlit hair blazed as intensely as her words.

"I'm sorry. I didn't mean to stare. It's just that—"

"That you're a guy. I know. They always—"

"No, Ms. Richards. They don't always do that. Not all of them." He looked down at the ground. "But when the sunlight hit your—"

"Yeah. I know. Looks like my hair's on fire. Kids at school used to tease me about it. They tormented me with obscene variations of *liar, liar, hair's on fire.*"

"I'll bet they don't do that anymore." He met her gaze and tried his most winning smile.

Her anger melted into a smile that won him completely. Her hint of a southern accent and a dozen other things about her sucked him in like a black hole pulls in asteroids. He needed to disappear from her life as rapidly as he entered it or she wouldn't be safe. Neither might Matt Mathison's heart.

"Matt? Where did you go? You're not on drugs, are you?"

"No. I don't use … drugs." His gut tightened.

"Spaced out on me?" She scraped mud from her hands on the tree beside the trail.

"Guess I did."

"You still haven't given me an explanation. Why did you sack me with that blindside blitz?"

She certainly had the football language down. It created an opportunity to tell her enough of the truth to keep her away from him, where it was safe.

Go on. Tell her enough to freak her out. You'll be doing her a big favor.

It wasn't what he wanted to do. He sighed. "There's someone who doesn't like me, Ms. Richards. I blindsided you because I thought you were him."

"Call me Randi. It's spelled with an *I.*"

"Okay. Randi with an *I,* you were running so hard, overtaking me, that I thought you were—"

"That I was the guy who wants to beat you up? For a few seconds I was the girl who wanted to beat you up. But you're safe ... for now." She grinned. "You know, if you're really worried about this guy, you should carry a gun."

He had a gun. Actually, three of them. But no one was supposed to find him here. Not for several months. When she ran down the trail like a wild Amazon, he just freaked out. "Yes. I could do that. But this guy doesn't know where I am." He paused. "Do you always run at that pace?"

She stared at him for a moment. Behind those glittering hazel eyes, the gears were turning. She knew he was hiding things.

If he could just tell her that he only hid them for her protection.

"Yeah. Used to run competitively, so I usually run hard. I warm up and stretch out before running. After a slow three hundred yards or so, if I'm feeling good, I kick in the after burners."

Good. She had recognized his change of subject and accepted it. And she did have afterburners. This young woman was an athlete. A perceptive one. The complete package. "I've been running out here for two months and have never seen another runner."

She laughed and again it sounded like music. "I've been running this trail for two weeks, and I've never seen anyone either. When do you usually run?" She knocked her shoe against a tree and a glob of mud fell off.

How much should he tell her? If the wrong person saw them together—he couldn't let that happen. "I run whenever I get the urge. Just about every day, except Sundays."

Randi squinted at his mention of Sundays, then relaxed. "I run to the big hill above the beach, take it easy down the steps, and run hard to the far end of Second Beach. I push hard back up those two hundred steps and give it all I've got back to the parking area. How far do you go?"

He smiled. "I run the same route, but a little slower on the return trip. What I'd like to know is how you caught me from behind on the way back without us passing on the trail."

Randi frowned, then broke into a smile. "Today I did something I've wanted to do since I got here. The tide was completely out, so I ran around the big rock at the far end of Second Beach. There's a hidden cove behind it that's cut off when the tide's in. I stopped there and explored for a few minutes."

"Do you mean that I made my turn, got at least three hundred yards ahead of you, and you still ran me down?"

"It appears so."

Matt was not dogging it today. He'd maintained a fast pace. She had to have world-class speed. He reran his quick calculation. Same conclusion.

"Hey, Matt ...." She twisted strands of her ponytail around her fingers. "Would ... uh ... you like to run with me on Monday? I always have this time slot free between my work tasks."

"I'd like that. But ... are you actually working today?"

Randi laughed softly. "Yeah. This and every day. I work a split shift, 4:30 to 7:00 each morning and evening, seven days a week."

"Seven days a week? Do you work at a dairy? Milk cows or something?"

"Milk cows?" She laughed again. "That's a good one. I don't know the first thing about farms, cows, living in the country, or—"

"What do you do in the middle of nowhere, on the edge of the Olympic National Park?"

"I'm a meteorologist. I send up the radiosonde at Quillayute and do a few other tasks at the weather station.

The weather observations are all automated except for the radiosonde."

"So you work for the National Weather Service?"

"No. They contracted out the weather services here a long time ago. The two men doing the work got tired of driving down from Port Angeles twice a day, so they hired me. It's my first job out of school."

He looked at the logo on her maroon and white shorts. "First job out of Texas A&M?"

"That's right. Gig'em, Aggies." She pointed both index fingers at the blue sky.

That explained the soft drawl.

"But this is miles from nowhere. Why are you—"

"I have my reasons, Matt." She gave him her laser look again. "Just like you have your reasons for hiding out here and jumping whenever you hear running feet."

"Got it." He smiled at her. "No more questions. Would you mind walking back to the parking area with me while we cool down?"

"Thought you'd never ask." She twisted her body and looked at her back side. "I still have a ton of mud caked on me in various places."

They turned and headed down the trail toward the parking area.

"Wait a sec." He twirled his index finger. "Turn around."

"What are you up to, Mr. Mathison?"

"Just checking you out."

"You've already done that ... thoroughly. I watched you."

"I meant checking to see how muddy you are before you get in a car."

She frowned. "If my shorts are a mess, it's all *your* fault."

"Hey. I've never tackled anyone *that* hard before. I was usually on the receiving end."

"Got tackled a lot, huh?" Randi nodded slowly. "Were you a running back or a quarterback?"

"Quarterback. But that was a lifetime ago." He wasn't ready to talk football, at least not about playing the game. "So, what do you think of the weather?"

She pointed up at the blue sky. "It's a strong El Niño. Otherwise we'd never see sunny and 68 degrees on April thirtieth at La Push."

"Ah, yes. I'm walking this trail with a meteorologist." He gave her a lingering look.

"And who am I walking with, if you don't mind me asking?"

He did mind, but he sought a truthful answer, at least one that told part of the truth. "I'm an unemployed, aspiring author. Nearly done with my first manuscript."

"A writer? We have something else in common. Running, writing and ... do you like 'rithmetic?" She laughed softly. "I started a novel once. Got the outline and two chapters done, then quit. What do you write?"

"Fiction. Romantic thrillers. It's not an official genre yet, but it's what I write."

She gave him several glances as they walked. "A romantic Lawrence Taylor or, should I say, John Elway? A man full of contradictions ... and secrets."

She was sharp. She'd even named *former* football stars. He had to be careful. This woman read him like a book and affected him in ways he didn't understand. She might pull his secrets out like a magician pulls a rabbit out of a hat, and he wouldn't have a clue how she'd done it.

Best not to attend her magic show. But he had already promised to run with her Monday. A bad idea, because each moment with her added to the magic.

A car door slammed in the parking area a hundred yards ahead.

He hooked her arm and yanked her off the trail behind some bushes.

"Matt, what are you—"

10

"Quiet," he whispered into her ear.

She stuck her head out the far side of the bush. "It's only the park ranger. He's probably checking out the trail." She studied his eyes. "I've got two questions for you, Matt. Who are you *really* afraid of? And ... is it safe for me to be here with you?"

Chapter 2

One twist of the handle on the tank and helium hissed into the big radiosonde balloon. It slowly billowed and lifted the weights at proper buoyancy. Off with the weights, out the door, and *bon voyage.*

Wait! Randi's fingers snagged the rising balloon. Good grief. She'd nearly forgotten to attach the transmitter.

Why were her hands and mind running on different tracks?

It was Matt's fault. His vague, evasive answers to her questions Saturday morning, like a bad cup of coffee, left a bitter taste in her mouth and spoiled her sleep.

She walked back into the launching shed outside the main weather station building and grabbed the transmitter.

A hand touched her shoulder.

She gasped and whirled.

Barely two feet away stood a man with leering brown eyes.

She jumped back, banging into the shed wall. "What are you doing here? This is private property."

"I did not mean to startle you. But was fascinated by you ... your ... by what you were doing."

Those eyes said he was more interested in her than her task. They made her skin crawl like she was covered with ants. "You haven't told me what you're doing here." Randi slid along the wall toward the filling station and rested her free hand on a brass weight.

He watched her closely, eyeing her hand on the potential weapon. "Perhaps you can help me."

Only if it gets you out of here.

"Perhaps. What can I do for you?"

"My amigo—my friend moved to this area. I was passing through and someone in town said he lives out this way. Mora Road or La Push. He's big, tall, dark hair, early twenties. Have you seen him?"

Was this guy describing Matt? No. Matt wouldn't know a creep like him. "I'm only out here when I work. Don't know many people. Sorry, I can't help you."

The wiry man's eyes flashed a strange glance at her. She couldn't read the emotions behind it, but it brought back the ants. A whole army of them.

"Thank you, sen—miss." He stepped back, turned and walked away, then disappeared around the corner of the weather building.

Randi stared at the corner of the weather station. She couldn't return to her task until she knew Igor had left.

An engine started. Gravel crunched on the driveway. He was gone.

If she never saw that man again, it would be too soon.

The time. She glanced at her watch. 5:05 a.m. The balloon launch would be more than five minutes late.

Randi attached the transmitter and moved outside to the launch point.

The big balloon rose into the blue-gray dawn sky. In about forty-five minutes, it would make its contribution to the numerical weather models.

Back to the business at hand. She needed to put the issue of Matt Mathison to rest.

Why did he have such an impact on her? He wasn't the first good-looking man she'd seen or been pursued by. But somehow, he was different.

Were her personal pain and loneliness taking their toll, making her vulnerable? That couldn't be. On the track, the other runners called her the ice woman. She could stare them down and run them into the ground. But when she stared at Matt, all the ice melted.

From somewhere deep inside a soft voice spoke, not so much words, but more like a feeling. Matt needed her.

Needs you? He just stopped talking to you and walked away.

He did walk away yesterday, leaving her two questions on the table, ignored and unanswered.

When they ran tomorrow—if Matt showed up—she would rephrase her questions from yesterday, bringing up her mysterious pre-dawn visitor, cast her bait into the water, and see if Matt bit. If not, there were other fish in the sea.

The straw in her cup gurgled, announcing the death of her latte. Randi slid out of her car and strode to the entrance of the little chapel.

Inside the door, a tall, broad-shouldered man, in a dress shirt and slacks, stood with his back toward her. He spoke with a middle-aged man.

The older man's focus switched to her. "Excuse me. I get the privilege of greeting a visitor."

The other man turned toward her. His eyes widened. "Randi?"

"Matt? What are you doing here?" Stupid question. The bright sunlight shining in through the chapel doorway must have fried her frazzled brain.

He grinned. "Probably the same thing you're doing. I came here to worship this morning."

She flung a hand upward. "Don't mind me. I just never learned what a church was for."

He scanned her head and grinned. "Liar, liar, hair's on fire."

"You're cruel, Matt." She gave him a mock frown.

The greeter waved his hand between Matt and Randi. "So, you two know each other?"

"Yes, Sam. I ran into her yesterday down by La Push."

"Literally. And I've got the bruises to prove it."

Sam squinted at Matt. "Well, aren't you going to introduce me?"

"Sam, this is Randi Richards ..." Matt paused, studied her face, and waited.

This was interesting. Asking permission. She nodded to Matt.

"She's a meteorologist. Randi, this is Sam Davenport."

"Hi, Sam. Glad to meet you."

So, Matt was considerate of her desire for privacy. She made another tally mark beside a growing total by Matt's name. Maybe she wouldn't have to wait until Monday to find out more about this intriguing, exasperating hunk of a man. She had never had a real boyfriend, never even kissed a guy. Why did Matt, a man with secrets, attract her like no one ever had?

Come on, Randi, you've never made a fool of yourself over any guy. Let's keep it that way.

The chiding words came from somewhere deep in the left side of her brain.

"But I'm right brain dominant," she muttered.

"What?" Matt cocked his head.

Great. He had heard her. "Nothing. I mean, the right side. I like to sit on the right side of the room. Is that okay?"

"Sure." He took her arm. "See you later, Sam. It's time for the service to start." Matt pulled her gently toward two seats in a vacant row on the right side of the chapel sanctuary and gave her a crooked smile. "Aren't you being a little presumptuous ... assuming that I would sit beside you?"

"No, I don't think so." She sat down and pulled him into the seat beside her. "Like yesterday, this isn't just a coincidence, you know."

His smile faded to a puzzled frown. "Do you always read meanings into things?"

"If the things are happening to me, yeah, I do. And thanks."

"For what?"

"For ... being considerate."

"Thank you, too."

"For what?" Randi cocked her head.

"Talking to me." He smiled warmly. "After I left yesterday, I wasn't sure you would."

"I think most people deserve a second chance, don't you?"

"The service is starting." Matt focused on the front of the room where the worship team had begun singing a chorus.

Déjà vu. What was that old song? *Yesterday Once More?* Or maybe he really did want to begin worshiping at that precise moment.

Randi tried to concentrate on the message of the worship songs as she struggled to sing melodies and lyrics that were new to her. And when Pastor Santos spoke, she tried to focus on the message. But with Matt beside her, and unanswered questions wedged between them, her success was spotty at best.

When the service ended, Matt immediately stood, shuffling his feet.

Apparently he wanted to leave. Now. No chatting with anyone, just walk away like he had done yesterday.

When his fidgeting intensified, and he appeared as if he might bolt and run, she caught his attention. "I don't have to be back to work until 4:30. Do you have any Sunday dinner plans?" What was she doing? She was supposed to be playing things cool.

"I'm sorry. Not today." He looked across the room at Pastor Santos, who was chatting with members of his congregation.

"Oh. I thought ... never mind. Does that mean you won't be running with me tomorrow?" Why had she added the last part? She was acting like a schoolgirl desperate for a boyfriend. Acting like a fool.

"No. I'll run with you." He avoided her eyes.

16

"Run with me, but not go to dinner with me?"

"Randi." He rubbed his forehead and brushed back his hair. "I've got to go."

"Fine. Go." She stepped into the aisle.

He strode past her and out the door.

She stared at the door. *He likes me. He likes me not.* Maybe she needed to find a daisy and start pulling off petals.

This man sent so many mixed signals it would take a crypto analyst to decipher them. Which was frustrating because Matt was someone she really wanted to get to know better. But unless he was willing to open up, there was no way she would let herself get emotionally attached to him. She'd already had enough hurt for the year. Maybe for the decade.

When she saw him tomorrow, she would force the issue. Matt would talk or she would walk.

* * *

Matt couldn't look back at Randi. His stomach already had a knife in it. Looking at her now would finish the job. Hara-Kiri.

The hurt, the pain on her face—he had inflicted that with his rude exit. She would take it as rejection. But, for her sake, he strode out the door of the church, around the corner of the building, out of sight ... and probably out of her life.

She would think he had left. Instead, he circled around to the back of the chapel, entered again through the side door, and headed for the pastor's office.

His life was a mess. He needed help.

Buck up, man. You've got some serious house cleaning to do.

He stepped inside the pastor's office, sat down in a visitor's chair, and waited.

Waiting wasn't a good thing. It made him think of Randi. Her laugh when she sat in the mud. Her blazing hair and twinkling hazel eyes. A beautiful woman who had secrets too. Maybe her own set of hurts. And she was probably lonely in this remote location.

In any other situation, he would be the one kicking in the afterburners ... in pursuit. But it *wasn't* any other situation, and anything he did involving Randi could put her in danger. Serious danger. The best thing he could do for all concerned was to get out of her life and get his life back on track. He wasn't fit to have a relationship with anyone right now.

The door swung open.

He jumped.

The pastor stepped in, looked into his eyes, and held out his hand. "It's good to see you, Matt." He had the firm grip of a straight shooter, a man Matt could trust.

"Thanks for making time for me when I'm sure you'd rather be eating Sunday dinner with your family."

The pastor rolled his chair out from under his desk and sat down. "No problem. My wife will keep something warm for me." He paused. "When you called, it sounded like you needed some advice and that privacy was paramount. How I can help you?"

How much should he reveal? Too much could endanger Pastor Santos. Too little, and he would be as bad off after the counseling as before—a balancing act where Matt had to walk a tightrope.

"Pastor, I've done some things. Fell so hard, so far, so fast, that I don't know if things will ever be the same between God and me ... and between other people and me. How do you find forgiveness after becoming a Judas?"

"A Judas? That's pretty harsh self-condemnation. Did you intentionally betray the Lord? Did you plan in advance to do it for personal gain?" He leaned forward, raised his eyebrows and waited.

Matt sighed. "Not exactly."

"Then you aren't a Judas, so don't use that metaphor."

Matt's shoulders raised in a weak shrug. "What metaphor should I use?"

"Try Peter. He denied his Lord three times while he was standing only a few feet from him. But Jesus forgave him and later made him a leader in that first congregation."

Matt nodded, but his intellect and his heart were not agreeing. Was that his problem? Did he trust his feelings even when they were at odds with theological facts? No. There had to be more to it than that.

"Matt?"

"Yes?"

"Thought I'd lost you there for a moment. Did you recommit your life after your, uh, fall?"

"Yes, and I meant it. I'm not going back to the other life. Ever."

Pastor Santos gave him a brief smile. "Good. Now here's something else you need to think about. To make things right, if you have hurt people, you need to ask their forgiveness, and you need to make restitution for anything you took from them."

Matt's head dropped until his chin bounced on his chest. He'd wronged a lot of people. The scope of his personal destruction was impossible to determine. "There are too many people to count, and I don't even know who most of them are."

Pastor Santos sighed sharply. "Okay, let's try a different tack. Did you violate any laws?"

"Yes. I committed some violations. Of the felony variety." He shook his head. Despite the pain that had driven him, he couldn't believe he'd been so stupid, so self-absorbed.

"Then no matter how hard it seems, you need to go to the appropriate law enforcement agency and tell them what you did."

"If I really want to clean up the mess I've made of my life, I know I have to do that. I was just hoping that ... maybe there was some other way."

The pastor's finger tapped out a snappy rhythm on the desk. "Another thing, Matt."

"You're really piling things on, pastor."

"No. We're clearing things off. If you take care of everything I've mentioned, to the best of your ability, you *will* start feeling a lot better. Gaining a clear conscience has a wonderful way of removing the gloom and depression that overwhelm us when we're carrying guilt." Pastor Santos nodded then shook his head. "But I don't want you just to *feel* better, Matt. Real forgiveness requires the complete removal of guilt by making full payment for the crime."

"Like spending time in prison." Matt's gaze dropped to the floor.

"In one sense, that's already been done for you. Christianity is the only faith where the crime was atoned for by the actual meting out of justice. A completely adequate payment was made for everything you've done wrong. Jesus was punished sufficiently for any crime a human being can commit."

"I know that theologically. But..." He pursed his lips and closed his eyes.

"Matt, if you want to *feel* forgiven, you need to rely on Jesus' payment as being adequate, to say it really *is* enough. With that reliance and the power of His Spirit active in your life, you can actually *be* better."

Matt raised his head and met the pastor's gaze. "You haven't told me anything I didn't already know."

"I didn't expect I would. Not if you're the young man I used to read about on the sports page a few years ago ...

20

the one everyone believed would take the Huskies to a national football championship."

If the pastor knew, how many other people knew also? "So you know who I was?"

"No. I see who you *are*. But do *you* know who you are, Matt? Look, I realize you're reluctant to disclose details about what you've done, so I can't give you any more detailed advice. But one thing you must *not* do—don't start trying to take care of your problem piecemeal. As much as possible, deal with everything you've done in one fell swoop. If it turns out you missed something, take care of it right then. No waiting."

Matt rubbed his throbbing temples. Thinking about what lay ahead gave him a worse headache than being targeted by a blitzing linebacker. He sighed. "But there is one piece that maybe I need to deal with separately, and I need your advice. I met Randi yesterday morning. She's the tall girl with the auburn hair who sat by me this morning."

"I noticed. She's a lovely young woman."

"For some strange reason, she likes me, or thinks she does. And I could more than just like her." He leaned forward, arms on his knees. "What should I do?"

"You need to tell her everything. You have no chance of a genuine relationship with her unless you do that."

"She hardly knows me yet. Shouldn't I wait a while before telling her my sordid story?"

"I wouldn't advise it. Secrets will always be exposed, eventually. If you conceal them, they will damage the relationship." Pastor Santos studied his face for a moment. "Until you're ready to tell me the details of what you're facing, I don't believe I can help you any further. Now, that being the case, do you want to schedule another appointment?"

Pastor Santos couldn't comprehend what he was asking. "Pastor, if I continue counseling with you, and tell you more, I might put your life in as much danger as mine is."

Chapter 3

At 6:45 a.m. the sun shone brightly above the Olympic Mountains to the east. Monday. Another sunny day in a long string of sunny days. The kind of weather that would lift anyone's spirits, unless they were Matt Mathison, the man about to shut Randi Richards out of his life forever.

He hopped in his truck and headed for the old Quillayute Airport, only three miles from his rented cottage. If she would ride to the trail head with him, that would give him more time to talk, to tell her enough so she would understand. After he'd walked away from her dinner invitation without replying, he wasn't sure what kind of reception he would receive.

She was obviously interested in him, and Randi seemed like the perfect girl. Perfect for him anyway. Unfortunately, she was the girl who came into his life at a perfectly wrong time.

The weather services sign mounted on a tall fence marked the turn. He pulled alongside the only car in sight, the one that had been parked at the Second Beach trail head on Saturday. It was parked by the only building on the WWII-era airstrip that wasn't in some state of collapse.

When Matt slid out of his truck, a tall, graceful silhouette rounded the corner of the weather station.

"Good morning, Randi."

She approached him, stopped two steps away, frowning as she studied him. Randi was dressed to run—a good sign. Her shorts and runner's tank top showed off a little extra muscle in all the right places. "I see you're talking again. You've walked away twice while I was talking to you. It won't happen a third time, Matt, or I'll—"

"You're right, it won't happen again. And about those two times—what I'm trying to say is, I need to explain some things to you."

Hands on hips now, she stared at him. "You need to explain a lot more than your rudeness."

"Ride with me to the Second Beach trail. If you'll run at a slower pace, we can talk while we run."

"I can slow things down if there's a good enough reason." She eyed him and an enigmatic smile tweaked the corners of her mouth.

"Am I a good enough reason?"

Matt, you're leading this woman on. You can't offer yourself like that. Not now.

He squelched the obnoxious voice.

Her arms relaxed and dropped to her sides. "Yeah. You're reason enough. Let me lock up, and we can leave."

Randi returned from the door and pointed at her car.

"We'll take my truck. No need for both of us to drive."

She wrinkled her nose. "That … thing?"

He jabbed a thumb at the truck. "Give it a chance. Don't judge a truck by its cover."

Randi glanced at the truck again. "I'll give it a try, as long as I don't end up as dirty as the last time we were on that trail."

"Not to worry." He opened the door for her.

As she climbed up and slid into the passenger's seat, her eyes widened. "Matt, this is incredible. The seats, the carpet, and, wow, what a stereo system."

"I sank a little money into the interior. Left the outside as it was. Pretty sure nobody's going to try to steal it. If they do, it's got a security system that will give them a big surprise."

They pulled out onto the road, and she gave him a sideways glance, waving a hand at the interior of his truck. "Does this relate to why you're hiding out here?"

"Partly. But I am a bit of an audiophile."

She nodded slowly. "Audiophile, huh? What do you listen to?"

"I have a big MP3 collection. Acoustic folk and, more recently, acoustic alternative Christian. Mostly indies. You probably wouldn't recognize their names."

She challenged him with her stare. "Try me."

"Okay. Andrew Peterson, Jill Phillips, Carolyn Arends—"

"Shall I pick it up from there?"

He chuckled. "If you think you can."

Randi gave him a smirky smile and counted on her fingers. "Ben Shive, Andy Gullahorn, After the Chase ..."

"But how did you—"

"Let's just say, we have similar tastes in music." She placed her hand on his right arm.

It was warm, like Randi's personality when it wasn't blazing. And they did have much in common, even their tastes in music. It would have been wonderful were it not for what was coming in a few minutes, when the dissonant music of his recent past pounded against her eardrums and the singer screamed the message that there were things they would never have in common.

The ache in Matt's gut turned to a nauseating knot, almost breaking his resolve. But he couldn't let that happen. No matter what, he must keep this beautiful, innocent young woman safe, even if it meant driving her away.

* * *

For the entire five-minute trip, Randi rested her hand on Matt's arm. His strength radiated from his arm to hers. Right now, she could use some strength and comfort, and Matt's arms seemed custom made for her needs. But did he want to help her?

Twice his arm moved upward, then stopped. He obviously wanted to take her hand. But he didn't.

What did that mean? She wouldn't have minded.

A warm, comfortable silence persisted between them. She didn't want to break it.

Evidently, neither did Matt.

But she did need to tell him about the creep who dropped by the weather station with a description that could fit Matt. That could wait a couple of minutes until they reached the trail. For now, silence was indeed golden.

After they parked, she slid out and propped a foot on the guard rail lining the parking area.

A few steps away, Matt did the same.

She pressed a forehead to her knee, held the stretch, then raised her head.

"I know it's necessary, but I hate stretching. Why don't you explain Matt Mathison to me and keep my mind off the drudgery?"

"So, I'm just a diversion in your life?"

Probing her thoughts again, while he hid his own. "Come on, Matt." She looked at him and slipped into a Spanish accent. "You got some 'splainin' to do."

His jaw tightened, and he sighed as if trying to relax. "I 'splain better while I'm running."

"Fine." She pulled her foot from the rail. "Since we're going to take it slow today, that's enough stretching. Let's go." She wheeled and jogged down the trail, assuming he would follow.

She'd left him no choice.

He followed.

"I can hear you better if you're behind me." She pointed a thumb back over her shoulder.

After she crossed the small bridge and began their ascent of the first hill, Randi spread the fingers of her raised hand and began a countdown, lowering one finger at a time. "Five, four, three, two, one ... you're on, Matt."

Silence.

Was this going to be like pulling teeth? "You know, Matt. The beginning is the best place to start. Just like in Genesis."

He took a deep breath, perhaps it was a sigh. "How old are you, Randi?"

What are you up to, Matt? She glanced back at him. "You know it's not polite to ask a woman her age. But then women are too sensitive about a lot of things. I'm twenty-two. How old are you?"

"I just turned twenty-four."

Silence again.

She glanced back.

Matt dodged an exposed root, took a deep breath, and blew it back out. "Genesis, chapter one. In the beginning, in the middle of your sophomore year in high school, I was the number-one-ranked high school quarterback in the nation. I had my pick of schools and chose the UW Huskies two months before National Letter of Intent day."

"Okay, top-rated quarterback. So what went wrong?"

"Hey, I'm telling this story," he huffed between breaths as they topped the hill and entered the deepest part of the forest. "The Huskies had a new coach and had their sights set on a national championship. Coach red-shirted me my freshman year to give him what he hoped were four good shots at the championship."

"How did you feel about that, not playing in any games your first year?"

"We agreed on it in advance, but at the end of my freshman year, in spring practice during the final scrimmage game ... I got hurt. Hurt really bad."

Serious injuries could be devastating to athletes. She had watched as it happened to others. And the timing of Matt's was the very worst. "That's awful, Matt." The words hardly expressed the anguish building inside her as Matt told his story. "What happened?"

"A blitzing linebacker blew out my right knee."

Her stomach tightened. She'd seen serious knee injuries.

"My weight immediately shifted to my left foot and a defensive lineman got that knee. At the same time, a big, strong safety hit me in the lower back." Matt paused and huffed a blast of air. "They blew out both of my knees, ruptured two disks in my back, and cracked one vertebra. Three freak accidents rolled into one. Nobody's fault, really … except maybe my offensive linemen for not picking up the blitz."

Randi slowed and stopped in the middle of the trail. The pain of his injuries, and the end of all his dreams, had come in a few seconds. Her eyes overflowed as she turned toward Matt.

He nearly ran into her. Matt grabbed her shoulders to prevent a collision.

She swiped her cheeks and wrapped her arms around him. "Matt, I can't imagine." She rested her head on his shoulder.

His arm slipped around her strong, but gentle.

Randi pulled her head back and looked at him through watery eyes.

His eyes softened. He removed his arms and brushed a tear from her cheek.

She took a calming breath then turned and jogged down the trail. "Did … did you ever play again?"

"I became a star player … in the OR. Had surgeries. Too many to count. The doctors said eventually I'd be able to do the things most people do, but no more contact sports, especially football. My scholarship was cancelled after a year."

Randi led them along the ridge line, still holding to a comfortable pace, still trying to wrap her mind around his horrific loss. "So what did you do after that?"

"There was a lot of pain. I used a lot of prescription drugs to get by. One day the doctor said I didn't need the drugs anymore. Maybe my body didn't, but my mind did. It had given up on life and wanted some kind of relief ... or escape. I managed to graduate, barely. And I eventually started buying my drugs on the street."

Drugs. On the street. Matt knew drug dealers. The man from yesterday... "Matt, the guy who's looking for you—does he have something to do with your drug days?" She knew the answer.

"Yes, indirectly."

An icy chill settled over her despite the warm, sunny morning. "I need to tell you something. Should have told you earlier, but..." She pulled Matt to a stop. "Yesterday morning, when I was preparing the radiosonde, a guy showed up at the weather station. He said he'd heard in town that one of his old friends lived out this way, near La Push or on Mora Road. The guy gave me a description that sort of fits you."

Matt's hands squeezed her shoulders. "Randi, describe the man."

"He looked Native American, possibly Hispanic. Medium height, a wiry build. His eyes gave me the creeps."

"Was he driving a black Hummer?"

"I don't know. He parked on the opposite side of the building. Is he the guy that wants to beat you up?"

"No." He blew out a blast of air. "He's the guy that wants to kill me."

Kill? Randi's mind began calculating the danger, danger to Matt and to her. The answer she computed frightened her.

"Randi, he's in this area. Anyone linked to me is in danger. I've got to get you back to your vehicle and go to the police for help. I ... I can't see you anymore."

"Wait, Matt, this isn't your fault. It just happened."

"But it *is* my fault. Don't you see? I brought this on myself. The man is a hired assassin. If he sees you with me, you could be killed too. I won't risk that."

"Can't the police help? I'll go with you, Matt. You don't have to do this alone."

"If the police got the FBI's assistance, maybe. But we can't be together, Randi. I couldn't stand it if ..."

She reached for his arm.

He pulled it away.

"Matt, don't walk away again. If you do—"

"But I have to. Let's go back to my truck and get you back to the airport."

He was doing it again. The picture of Matt became clear in her mind. He would always do this. She would never be a part of his life

Randi bolted toward the trail head. But it wasn't her car parked there, it was his truck. No matter. She could run all the way back to the airport.

First her parents deserted her, and now Matt. Right now, running was the only thing that could keep her from falling apart.

Matt's driving steps sounded behind her. He was sprinting to catch her.

That wasn't going to happen. Randi accelerated into an all-out sprint. Matt would not stop her. Not now. Not ever.

The pounding feet behind her came at a furious pace.

She kept sprinting, oblivious to everything but those driving footsteps close behind her.

He caught her at the top of the hill where the trail descends to the trail head. Matt grabbed her arm and yanked.

She ripped it away and continued to run.

"Randi, stop. This is dangerous."

She ran hard, pulling away from him. "You're not going to walk away from me again. Goodbye, Matt."

* * *

From the hill, Matt glanced to the parking area nearly 200 yards ahead. A bolt of lightning shot through his nervous system.

A black Hummer sat next to his truck.

Randi didn't seem to notice. She was rebuilding her lead.

Matt sprinted all out until Randi was within reach again. When he leaned forward, flying heels from her true runner's stride nearly kicked him in the chest. He backed off and again glanced toward the trail head.

The wiry form of a dark-complexioned man moved onto the trail. Zambada. He clutched a gun in one hand. Probably an assault rifle, an AK-47, the weapon of choice among cartel members.

As if oblivious to the danger ahead, Randi topped the hill one-hundred fifty yards from the parking area and ran directly toward the gunman.

Matt lunged and snagged the back of her spandex top.

As she accelerated down the trail, the fabric stretched like a rubber band.

His fingers slipped.

The strap snapped her in the back. She flinched, turned her head, and glared at him. "Leave me alone, Matt. That hurt."

"Stop, Randi! It's him!"

With her eyes focused on the descending trail, she couldn't see the man.

Zambada raised his weapon.

Matt dove for Randi. He wrapped her up in his arms and legs rather than driving through her. His coach would have scolded him for the soft tackle, but it was effective. He took her down and rolled onto the right edge of the trail.

Randi struggled to break free from his arms.

The staccato popping of an assault rifle echoed through the trees.

Matt's nostrils burned from the pungent smell of shredded spruce.

Randi gasped. She'd finally recognized the danger.

The gunman fired a second burst. Bark, limbs, and leaves exploded into the air a foot above Matt's head, trimmed by Zambada's deadly pruning machine.

They rolled off the trail to the right and the gunman lowered his aim to the ground as another burst of gunfire sounded. Dirt exploded upward filling, the air around them with clouds of dust.

Randi's trembling arm circled his neck.

More gunfire sounded, and a line of flying dirt zipped along the trail directly at them.

Matt pulled hard and flung Randi farther to their right.

She landed behind a large windfall, a temporary shield from the bullets coming eight-per-second at them.

Still exposed, he crawled toward the downed tree that protected Randi.

The line of bullets crossed his path a split second before he reached cover.

An intense sting sent muscles into spasms, screaming its pain throughout his left arm. Though he'd been hit, he continued forward until he rolled onto Randi, smothering her body with his.

When the popping stopped, she was sobbing. "I'm so sorry, Matt. I didn't believe you, didn't trust—"

"It's okay." His muscle spasms eased to a pulsating pain. This woman, in mortal danger, was more worried about doubting him than about the gunman who was only seconds from blowing them away. "When I say run, go straight ahead into the trees, away from the trail."

She nodded, wiping her eyes. "Then you need to get off me."

The throbbing intensified as he rolled off. He glanced at his arm. A stream of blood ran from a long, shallow wound in his triceps. An inch to the right and he would have lost an arm. Might have bled out, leaving Randi alone to face Zambada. Matt had to prevent that at all costs.

A metallic click replaced the shooting sounds

Zambada was changing the magazine. It would take three to four seconds.

"Run." He pulled Randi up and shoved her away from the trail.

They ran pell-mell into the forest, leaping over decaying logs and skirting bushes in the open areas.

The belching of the assault rifle sounded again and Zambada pruned more vegetation.

Particles of wood stung the back of Matt's neck as the pungent odor of evergreens filled the air. "Run. We've got to go faster. Need more separation."

"Then we should circle back to the trail so we can really run." She was thinking … shrewdly.

It brought him an idea and a sliver of hope. "Which way to the dogleg where we collided?"

She dodged a tree and pointed due west. "About one hundred yards."

Randi circled that direction before he could voice his suggestion. Tough, smart, and could perform under pressure. But her breathing had turned to panting.

"You sound tired. Can you make it?"

"I'm fine. Too much excitement … hyperventilating."

"Have you got a fast mile left in you?"

She flashed him a weak smile over her shoulder. "You know me, always good for one more mile."

"When we hit the trail, sprint all out toward the beach and we can gain two or three, hundred yards on him."

"The beach? That isn't a good idea. It's a dead end."

"But *he* doesn't know about the beach. When we get far enough ahead, we'll circle back through the woods. Try to reach my truck."

Randi pushed through the boughs of a tree and ran out onto the trail.

He followed as she accelerated along the ridge line toward the beach. Though he was sure they were far ahead, Matt glanced back at the dogleg. Far beyond it, through a narrow gap in the trees, he caught a glimpse of Zambada loping along the trail, both hands on his weapon.

The assassin's head snapped up and the two made eye contact. Even at this distance Matt was sure of it.

Zambada switched the gun to one hand and accelerated to a sprint, toward them.

Matt flanked Randi. "He saw us."

She stepped up the pace. "Let's sprint to the top of the steps and hide in the trees?"

"Won't work. The forest opens up too much there. He's not far enough behind. He'd gun us down." They couldn't afford to make detrimental concessions "We have no choice. We've got to increase our lead. The only way is to run down the hill and onto the beach."

"Matt, the ocean's on one side, the cliff on the other." Randi took several deep breaths. "The beach dead ends. We'll be trapped."

He ran up close behind her. "Randi?"

No response.

He drew to her side. "Look at me."

She glanced at him. Terror now shone from her wide hazel eyes.

He wanted to erase it. To never see it again. But all he could offer was a gamble with long odds. "Trapped or not, we don't have a choice."

"There's got to be another option."

"Yeah. We could stop right here and let him shoot us?"

The trail widened, but Randi stuck close to his side. "No. Race you to the beach, Matt."

Chapter 4

Randi slowed as she approached the hill above the beach. This is where they could afford no mistakes, or they'd end up trapped. "Once we hit the beach, how do we shake this guy?" She spoke between heavy breaths.

"Let me think for a minute."

"Can't. We hit the steps in less than sixty seconds."

Matt adjusted his stride to match hers. "When's high tide this morning?"

"In two hours. It's probably starting its big surge about now." She swallowed hard. "Are you thinking about the cove?"

"I know it's a gamble."

She shook her head. "You got that right." But what if the gunman couldn't be sure they were on the beach? "I've got an idea. We run hard down the steps. Leave no tracks on the beach. Then we hide in the cove and wait."

He gave her thumbs up. "But how do we avoid leaving footprints in the sand?"

With the steps looming ahead, she didn't reply.

Matt ran ahead of her as they approached the top of the nearly two hundred steps carved into the hillside, descending to the beach. As she suggested, he ran hard, taking most of the steps two at a time.

But it seemed they were going too slow. "Matt, let's try three at a time."

He stretched out into a three-step rhythm.

Good. They flew by the bushes and trees along the trail, descending the steep hill in long, bounding strides.

After the second switchback, Matt slowed, taking more time to hit each step.

She moved as close behind him as she dared, while concentrating on keeping her rhythm.

Matt took two steps, then three, then two and his body pitched forward.

She grabbed a handful of his T-shirt and reared back with all of her strength.

They both landed on their rear ends with apparently nothing worse than sore fannies.

"I almost lost it. Thanks." Blood oozed from a clot on Matt's triceps.

The dark red flow stopped her heavy breathing. He'd been shot? And he hadn't even said anything.

Matt yanked her to her feet.

"You're hit, Matt. I didn't know. I—"

"It's nothing serious. Thanks for saving me from a nasty fall, but we gotta keep moving."

Saved him from a fall? Nothing like what he saved her from when he was hit by automatic weapon fire. Maybe there was a lot more to this man than she had suspected.

Randi slowed the pace for the rest of the descent, taking two steps at a time.

After reaching the bottom, she pulled Matt to the bushes on their right, toward the creek that flowed beside the trailhead. "Follow it to the surf."

Thank goodness the little creek hadn't dried up from the drought. Their shoes might get wet and sandy but, if they followed it into the surf, they would leave no visible tracks.

When they reached the ocean water, Randi continued ahead, plunging into the waves.

"Smart girl," he yelled over the surf.

"Only if we round the bend before he reaches the beach, and then run the half mile to the point. If we can slip around it and get into the cove without being seen or bashed against the rocks, we might be safe." She picked up the pace, splashing through waves. Sand now filled her shoes. With nearly a half mile to go, it would soon produce blisters or abrasions.

In less than a minute, they reached the bend. Her feet were killing her.

Randi glanced back before the trailhead sign disappeared from view.

A figure stumbled out of the bushes at the trailhead and hopped onto the driftwood logs. The gunman. He turned their way just as they passed out of sight around the bend.

Had he seen them? She wasn't going to stop to find out.

After running another fifty yards, the pain from her feet, enhanced by the saltwater, slowed her to a limping trot. She slowed further and ripped off her shoes. "Don't ruin your feet, Matt. We need them."

"Wasn't going to say anything, but mine are killing me."

"Yeah. They could kill us. That's what I'm afraid of."

He yanked his shoes off, then touched her arm as they resumed their run. "Your plan is a good one. I trust you, Ran."

Ran. Matt had shortened her name like guys did when— she didn't have time for that kind of speculation.

But even before having a chance to hear his story, she trusted Matt. Trusted that he would do his best to keep her safe. He had taken a bullet for her. She could trust him with her life. Despite their situation, knowing she was in his hands, under his protection, brought more comfort than Randi had experienced in months.

Fifty yards ahead, the tall rock at the end of the beach guarded the point like a giant sentry. Waves battered it, sending foaming water high onto the rock. The incoming tide appeared to be around four feet deep at the point. Could they get around it safely? Or, would the sentry keep everyone out? They had no choice but to try.

"We've got to hurry, Matt. This isn't a cinchy thing."

Matt waded out into the icy water. "I'll go first. If something happens to me, you—"

"No way, Matt Mathison. If something happens to you, I'd be left alone with that creep." She grabbed his hand. "We go together or not at all."

He squeezed her fingers. His hand was big, warm, and strong. With a killer trailing them, she needed Matt for—for maybe too much.

"Let's start in the backwash of the next wave." He motioned toward a rising swell.

The big wave rushing at them broke and roared, then rolled toward shore, giving their pathway around the rock a sinister look. The wave was the pestle, the big rock was the mortar, and they were the grain.

She stepped close to Matt and pointed ahead.

Matt met her gaze. The intensity in his eyes softened for a second. He glanced at the wave passing them, then tugged on her hand. "Let's go."

She followed as he tried to sprint, impeded by three feet of water and the backrush that sucked them seaward. The water rose to the top of her thighs when they reached the point, and the next wave broke less than fifty feet from them. The ominous roar gave strength to her churning legs.

They made the turn and headed toward the cove.

The wave slapped them in the back, nearly knocking her down.

They ran with the wave's current, but when they reached shallow water, Matt pulled her to a stop. "To be safe, let's not leave any tracks in the sand here. Climb on the sides of the rock until we reach the rocky part of the cove."

"Good idea. If he somehow manages to stick his head around the corner, we can at least partially hide, so ..."

"So he won't blow us away."

"Don't say it, Matt. That's not going to happen."

"You're right. He wouldn't try rounding that point without a really good reason. We haven't given him a reason, have we?"

Randi shrugged. "I ... I saw him jump out from the trailhead just as we rounded the bend, but—"

"Did he see us?"

"I couldn't tell." She scampered along the side of the rock ahead of Matt. "The tide's coming in strongly now. It's already a foot deeper than when we came around the rock." She reached the small, rocky portion of the beach above the high tide mark. "It's too late for our friend even to try now. Look." She pointed at the waves crashing against the rock where the water was now over five feet deep.

Matt smiled. "I almost wish he would try about now."

She looked higher up on the rock. The face was a smooth, nearly a vertical cliff. Still the thought of that ruthless killer climbing around the rock hit her like a punch in the stomach, bringing nausea. She stepped close to Matt, took his hand and squeezed it. "But what if he does come? What do we do?"

He looked into her eyes, studying them.

He could probably see the terror there, a kind of terror she'd never faced before. It sent her heart racing without pumping enough blood, without providing enough oxygen. She panted trying to catch her breath.

"Randi, don't worry. He's not going to make it through the surf. But if, somehow, he scales the rock ... I'll take him out."

"Take him out? Matt, *he's* the one with the gun."

"They used to call my arm a cannon. Pretty accurate too." Matt selected three baseball-size rocks and another larger one. "He'll need both hands to hold onto the rock. He won't be able to shoot. Not right away. Before he gets the chance, I'll take his head off with one of these."

Standing beside him, she slipped an arm around his waist and glanced up.

Matt's gaze riveted on her face while he hooked an arm around her.

What she saw in his eyes any other time would have taken her breath away. Maybe this wasn't the time for those kinds of feelings, but there was no denying that she had them.

A metallic clank sounded between the crashing of waves.

Matt's head jerked toward the big rock. He dropped his hand from her waist, scooped up a rock, and stood like a pitcher throwing from the stretch. "He's climbing around it. We've got two choices—squeeze back into the corner of the cove and pray he goes back without seeing us, or I nail him as soon as he appears on the rock face."

Another clank sounded, followed by the sounds of shoes rasping on the rock face, just beyond the corner.

Chapter 5

Randi locked her gaze on the corner of the towering rock. The gunman's head could pop around the corner any second. That thought sent her stomach churning.

Matt stood, rock in hand, studying the corner of the monolith. "The face is almost vertical. I didn't think he could climb it."

She caressed Matt's injured arm. Touching him calmed her. "Matt, he wouldn't be so persistent unless he saw us on the beach, would he?" She spoke softly, letting the waves damp out the sound of her voice.

Matt shook his head. "I'm not sure. He could be just grasping at straws. But more likely he saw us, then we disappeared around the bend. When the tide cut him off, it probably made him mad."

The clattering grew louder, more frequent. A voice sounded between the waves, yelling out some foreign word.

Randi squinted from the bright sun as she looked up at Matt. "*Deeto*? Is that what he said?"

"Not exactly. I won't give you a literal translation. Suffice it to say he's very upset and has a place in mind that he wants send us to."

"So the poor little assassin is upset." She shivered.

A loud scraping sound, followed by a cry and a loud splash. Several more *deetos*.

Matt's face broke into a big grin.

"I take it that multiple *deetos* transcends upset. Falling into forty-eight-degree water can do that to a person."

Matt set his rock back on the ground and hooked an arm around her. "His gun's wet and full of sand. He can't use it until he cleans it. He's cold and—"

Another cry came along with splashes in the water.

Matt chuckled softly. "I think that wave got him. Sounds like he's wading out."

"Could you tell what else he was saying?"

42

"Something about returning. He's going back, leaving the beach. He must not have seen us come in here or he wouldn't have given up on this spot."

She looked high above them at the cliff overhanging the cove. "What if he takes another path? Could he see us from up there?"

Matt shook his head. "I've been up there. He can't get close enough to the edge to see the cove. If he tries, he'll slide off and the one-hundred-foot fall will kill him."

"So were safe for a while?"

"For now."

She looked up at Matt and smiled warmly. "It worked. The hidden cove hid *us*."

When he looked down into her eyes, what she saw in his stole her words and stole her breath.

Matt pulled her gently to him. "I couldn't let him hurt you. Even though we just met a few days ago, I'd do anything—"

She pressed her fingers over his lips. "You *did* everything, Matt. You shielded me with your body, took a bullet that I couldn't have avoided."

He brushed a stray lock of hair from her cheek. Dropped his hand to the back of her neck, nudging her closer. Even as he tried to kiss her, he was allowing her to opt out.

That's not going to happen.

She pulled Matt's head toward her, pressed her lips to his, and became lost in the soft, sweet kiss until she slowly pulled her lips from his.

Her first real kiss. It wasn't born of impulse. This moment had been more than two days in the making, but what would come next? Randi was all out of words and didn't want some stupid remark to slip out of her mouth as it too often did, so she kissed him again.

When he ended the kiss, his gaze sought hers. "I hope you didn't mind ..."

"Matt Mathison, I would have minded a lot if you hadn't."

Her face, still warm from his kiss, now felt hot.

He peered deeply into her eyes again. "You know, we're stuck out here for at least four hours, until the tide turns and goes half way out."

"You said he couldn't see us from above, but do you think he'll wait on the beach?"

"We might run into him when we leave, depending on where he's looking at the time."

"Matt, why is he trying to kill us?"

He sighed, hooked an arm around her waist, took her to a flat spot on the side of the big rock, and sat down with her. "The man's name is Zambada, with an emphasis on the b-a-d. He's a hit man working for a Mexican drug cartel. He wants to kill me because I left the organization."

"Why is he shooting at me then?"

"He wants to kill you because you're with me. That's why I was avoiding you. I didn't want to endanger you."

Maybe the events of the morning had sent her mind into a tizzy. She wasn't following his logic. "But you ran with me this morning and that *did* endanger me."

"I planned to tell you today that I couldn't see you anymore."

"Were you really going to do that to me?" A lump formed in her throat, and she barely croaked out the words.

He cupped her cheek. "Not *to* you. *For* you."

She waved off his words with her hand. "Forget what you intended this morning. What about now?"

"Isn't that obvious? But you're already in danger. So we've got to decide what to do about it. We'll have to go to the police, and I'll tell them my story."

"Were you really part of a Mexican drug cartel?"

"Not exactly."

"That was a little vague, Matt." She scooted away from him and met his gaze. "After being shot at and running so hard I nearly puked, don't you think you owe me a full explanation of what's going on?"

"Yes, I do." He took a deep breath and exhaled slowly, his gaze on the brilliant, blue water stretching to infinity in front of them. "I lost everything when I couldn't play football, Ran. Even the desire to go on living. That's when the father of lies started pushing Matt Mathison's buttons."

Matt didn't seem the kind of guy to finger-point. "You can't blame it all on him."

"I don't. It's my fault. But the realization that I could make a lot of money by *selling* drugs instead of *using* them was a big temptation. At that low point in my life, it was one I couldn't resist."

She looked down at the rocks by their feet, shaking her head. "Didn't you think about all of the lives you were destroying?"

"I did after I'd set up my first big drug deal. That deal showed me that the fortune I had planned to make playing football in the NFL could be made another way. All my dealing was to be done under the auspices of the reformed Tijuana Cartel. After that deal caught the attention of the high mucky-mucks in the cartel, they called a meeting. The head guy kept his distance. Watched from a hill three hundred yards away. The cartel's second in command made me an offer to become a mucky-muck, an offer I couldn't refuse."

Yeah, sure. Just like the mafia in a Hollywood movie. "That's not true. You could have just said no."

"Randi, by then I knew too much about them, their organization, how they operated, and after the meeting, I knew who the leaders were. Either I joined them, toed the line, and lived, or I refused their offer and got chopped up with a machete."

"So you said yes? That easily?"

"I told *them* I accepted it. Said it was an honor to be counted worthy of their trust. Then I hid money away in various bank accounts and tried to become invisible. So here I am, hiding and trying to put my life back together."

She had more questions and opened her mouth to voice them.

"Before you ask me anything else, let me finish. I refused your offer of dinner Sunday because I had an appointment with Pastor Santos right after church. I asked him what I should do with my messed-up life ... and what I should do about you."

"About me?"

He took her hand. "I wanted to spend time with you, to get to know you, but I couldn't tell you because I was so afraid of endangering you. And now my worst fears have been realized. You're in danger because of me."

Randi shook her head. The shake slowly morphed to a nod. "Matt, despite the danger and the fear, I can't think of any place I'd rather be than with you."

"Don't be so quick to say that. There's more."

"Are the police after you too? You broke some laws."

"That's the other part the pastor advised me about. I need to turn myself in."

Another element of uncertainty in Matt's future, in hers. "I agree, though I can't say it will be easy." She reached for his hand but stopped, resting it on the rock between them. "And what did the pastor say to do about me."

Matt sighed and looked into her eyes. "He said to do what I'm doing now—tell you everything and accept your response, whatever it may be."

"You've seen my response, Matt."

"No. The kiss came before you heard the truth about me." He looked away. "About how low I sank."

"Do you need a repeat to convince you?" She lifted her chin.

"Need one to believe you? No. Want one? That's another matter." He took her hand from the rock.

She scooted back near him, aware of her quickening pulse. How could she be sitting beside a confessed drug dealer—well, a would-be drug dealer—with her stomach doing flip flops and her heart doing double time? She smiled at him, squeezed his hand, and shook her head. "Can you believe it? We're in a hidden cove discussing necking like a couple of teenagers while a hired assassin is somewhere in the vicinity trying to blow us away?" She giggled softly. "It'll be quite a story to tell our—"

Her face warmed. The words had just come out from somewhere in her subconscious, or her soul—wherever the real Randi Richards resided. "Sorry, I don't know why ..." She studied his eyes and face. The haunted look and the mystery she'd seen before had vanished from his eyes.

"I refuse to comment on the grounds that it may tend to incriminate me."

She leaned her head on his shoulder and interlaced the fingers of their clasped hands "But when you go to the police, you *will* have to incriminate yourself. After that, what will happen to you, to us?"

"You'll need protection, Ran. The next few days, or weeks, will tell us how *much* protection. I may get my protection in jail."

"I was talking longer term than that."

"I couldn't ask anyone to be the girlfriend or wife of a felon."

"Please, don't do this again. You're a good man, Matt. You're not a felon."

"Oh, I'm a felon alright. Just an unconvicted one. Because I've gotten things right with God doesn't release me from getting things right with the law. It does just the opposite. I want a clean slate, Ran. A spiritual *tabula rasa.*"

She raised her head and looked into his face, seeking assurance. "Don't they drop the charges when people voluntarily come forward? If you worked to help them take down the drug dealers?"

"Sometimes. But there's no guarantee."

"There's only one guarantee I want. I ... I can't give my heart away to anyone unless I've got a commitment from them that they're not going to walk away and break it. Because when that happens, there are a lot of tears. And tears make a lousy lullaby."

His eyes had a soft look. "Are you speaking from experience?"

"Yes."

"I'm sorry."

"It was my roommate's experience at college."

His shoulders relaxed. "So you haven't had *your* heart broken?"

"Not by a guy. Only by ..." She pushed off the rock to stand. "You know, we should be making plans to get out of here."

He still held her hand and tugged gently until she sat back down. "We have at least three hours to make plans. But first you need to tell me about your broken heart and why you're hiding out here on the Peninsula."

What he asked was a fair question. But her answer would sound so weak, so unimportant, compared to his dramatic story.

"Whatever it was, it obviously hurt you deeply. Please tell me."

There was such a warmth in his eyes that she couldn't refuse his request. Randi leaned her head on his shoulder and stared out to sea. Except for the waves on the shore, it was a calm sea, unlike her family life.

"My mom is a professor at the University of Chicago in their Biological Division. Dad is a physicist at Argonne National Labs. Mom bought into the Neo-Darwinian orthodoxy, swallowed the whole thing, and was constantly pushing it onto me. Dad's more of an agnostic. I'm not sure what he thinks deep down inside, but he lets Mom have the final say if it relates to worldviews."

"But you're a Christian. Is that the problem?"

"It shouldn't be, but it is. I didn't want to follow in my parent's atheistic, agnostic, or professional footsteps. And I didn't like the Chicago area. So I went off to school at Texas A&M to study Meteorology."

"Why did you choose A&M?"

"Good Meteorology department, warm climate, and a long way from Chicago. I was a seeker, Matt. Still a bit of an agnostic. I came to faith during my junior year after getting involved with a Christian organization on campus. When I told my parents, Mom basically disowned me. Dad—" Her voice broke. "He wouldn't stand up *to* her or *for* me." Randi wiped away the tears that had escaped.

Matt curled an arm around her shoulders.

Knowing someone wanted to be close to her eased the pain. If only she could always count on him to be there for her. She took a deep breath. "They didn't attend my graduation. Just sent me one of those blank cards that you write something in. They said I should take all my things from the house and leave until I came to my senses."

Tears flowed again. She couldn't stop them. Her arms were around him now. Holding onto Matt helped her handle the ache inside.

Randi drew a calming breath. "If you really cared about your kids, if you were concerned about what they were doing, wouldn't you want them close to you? Wouldn't you want to be a good influence on them? But with Mom, I think it's a pride thing. Christianity won, and she lost, so she kicked me out."

"Ran, that was brutal. After that kind of rejection you probably—"

"Yeah. I have a hard time with rejection of any sort. I don't go out of my way to be accepted, but rejection hurts."

Matt pulled her closer. "So when I walked away from you ..."

"Yeah. It hurt, Matt."

"But you gave me more chances, even asked me to dinner."

"If you weren't so thick-headed, that should have told you a lot." She raised her head and watched his eyes, smiling as she wiped away more tears.

He kissed her forehead and held her as she listened to the waves, the gulls, and felt the warm sunshine on her skin.

"I'll never reject you." His voice grew soft. "No matter what happens or what I have to do, I won't reject you."

* * *

Randi's words replayed in his mind, "I can't give my heart to anyone unless I've got a commitment that they're not going to walk away and break it."

Those words ripped Matt's heart to shreds. How could he promise her he wouldn't walk away when there were so many uncertainties? If leaving kept Randi alive, he would be gone in an instant. A woman like her would find a good man to love, and she would find happiness. But that was predicated upon her being alive. Any option which put her in serious danger, but improved his chances of being with her, was no option at all.

Despite his promise, Matt had to tell her. And it had to be soon.

Chapter 6

The tide had turned, and Matt watched it slowly receding. Time to finalize their plan to elude Zambada. But it would take both of them working together as a team to escape.

"Randi, we need to talk."

She studied his eyes.

He feared they had betrayed him.

Hers widened with shock, then filled with tears. Finally, they glared with the anger of deep hurt. "You're doing it again, Matt." She turned away.

She had done it again too. Read him like a book. She knew what was coming. "Randi?"

"I'm not Randi. My name's Miranda. Call me Miranda."

"Miranda? I thought it was Randi with an 'I'."

"It is ... or was. My birth name is Miranda." Her voice was on the ragged edge of breaking.

"Why did you start using Randi?"

"Because I *hate* Miranda."

"But you want me to call you—"

"Yes."

Hate the name so she can hate the name caller? She'd gotten her point across, though it seemed a childish way to do it. He could play that game too. "I guess it's true, fiery hair, fiery temper."

"Matt, you're making fun of my hair. I told you never to do that!"

"Hush, he might hear us."

She stopped yelling and hid her face in the corner of the cove, against the big rock. Her body shook with each muffled sob.

Now what? He couldn't stand it when women cried. But this wasn't just any woman, and he had inflicted her pain by putting her life at risk, then her heart.

Sometimes Matt Mathison seemed incarcerated in the left side of his brain where logic ruled. Maybe it was time for a jailbreak.

He wanted to hold Randi and comfort her, but he wasn't sure what reception his arms would receive.

She stiffened and stopped sobbing when his feet crunched on the rocks behind her.

"Ran?" He stepped near and reached for her. The blood clot cracked, and a trail of blood rolled down the front of his arm only inches from her face.

Randi drew a sharp breath, then looked up into his eyes.

Not knowing what to expect, he studied her eyes for a clue. They were filled with tears, but the pain in them had changed to something else, something he couldn't discern.

"I need to tell you something, Ran. With my uncertain future, it isn't—"

"Everyone's future on this planet is uncertain."

"But what if the person dies and—"

"What if he doesn't? Isn't it better to plan for the future you really want and reach for it even though you might fail?"

He couldn't argue with her logic. He didn't want to. But he had to for her sake. "Ran, I think—"

"You think you're unselfishly protecting me. I know you, Matt. After three days I know you a lot better than you think. But unselfish means putting what someone else wants ahead of what you want. Do you even *know* what I want, Matt?"

"The tide has turned. We need to firm up our plan for getting back to my truck."

"Stop changing the subject. We'll come up with a plan, and it will be a good one. But first tell me what *you* think I want." She challenged him with glaring watery eyes.

With her flushed cheeks, chest heaving with emotion, and hair on fire from the bright sunlight, this woman, who clearly wanted a serious relationship with him, had a beauty he couldn't even describe with his English major's vocabulary.

"Matt?"

He sighed in resignation. "You want me to explain what I'm planning to do and why ... and you want us to discuss it before I charge off on my own."

"And?"

"And I think you really want to be with me, despite the danger and the uncertainty."

A faint smile graced the corners of her mouth.

"So you're waiting to hear what *I* want?"

"And how you feel. You nearly choked when you tried that a few minutes ago." She stepped close, inches away.

Randi's face, eyes, and hair filled his field of view. His left-brain logic was useless against the physical presence and the exposed heart of Randi Richards.

Matt raised his hands to hold her.

She raised an eyebrow.

He pulled his hands back to his sides.

The words. He needed to say them. "I ... I don't know everything about you, and this sounds crazy, but it feels like I've known you forever—like I've been looking for you for a long time—and I care about you, Ran. A lot."

She smiled as tears spilled onto her cheeks.

For the first time in years, Matt had let down his defenses and exposed his heart. Would he regret it?

Randi rested her head against his neck and shoulder. Her words, spoken softly, blended with the waves of the ebbing tide. "I care about you too, Matt. After today, we don't know what our future holds, but I believe we can make it through anything if we stick together."

He held her snugly, trying to make her feel loved and protected. But her protection needed to be more than just a feeling.

The tide had done enough ebbing. Now he had to get her safely off this beach. "We need a plan to get out of here. I've got an idea, but it's a bit dicey."

Chapter 7

Matt studied the water level at the point and the size of the incoming waves. He and Randi could get around the point without being bashed against the rock.

She glanced at the point then looked up at him and raised her eyebrows.

"Looks like we can go now, Ran. But there are two risky parts to this. First, when we round the corner of the rock, if he spots us, we've got big trouble and no place to hide. Second, we can't let him see us running down the beach. If he does, we might get lucky and elude him, but I'd rather not depend on luck."

She nodded. "So we've got—"

"We've got a risk reduction problem, and I've got the first part covered." He moved to the water's edge. "Come here."

After she stepped beside him, Matt draped an arm around her shoulders.

"See that rock sticking up above water about ten feet to the left of the point?"

"Yeah. But, Matt, the water's cold."

"I know. But I can stand it for a minute or so. The sun will warm me up when I get out."

She frowned at him. "Pretty sure I'm a stronger swimmer than you. Swam on our high school team."

"Ran, look at you. You're so ... well, I've got more body mass and more insulation."

"Are you insinuating that I'm like that beanpole ... what's her name?"

"Olive Oil?"

"That's not who I was thinking of. But you're no Popeye, either."

"But my body has more mass than yours. Less chance of hypothermia."

That piercing look. He must have left something unsaid during their Popeye-the-Sailor-Man digression. "Uh, Ran, you're in great shape."

"But you think I run too much don't you? You think I'm too scrawny and—"

"What I think is that we should focus on getting out of this cove, not on your vital statistics."

"Vital to me but not to you, is that what you're saying?"

This sounded like more rejection phobia. It was also a verbal land mine.

"Randi, you're perfect. But your hair's red. My dark hair will blend with the rock, and he won't see me unless he has high-powered binoculars focused on that rock when my head pops up."

"What if you see him?"

"I'll see if I can determine what he's doing, then swim back under water."

"What if you don't see him?"

"I motion for you to come around the rock. Then we run and hide in the bushes at the base of the cliff."

"Sounds good. Have you ever noticed the small creek that comes off the cliff about seventy-five yards from here?"

"I think so. Why?"

"Let's climb the cliff there. We can probably find enough bushes and scrubby trees along the creek to pull ourselves up the draw and into the forest."

Her smile. Her hair blazing in the sun. He couldn't stop staring at her. And she certainly wasn't Olive Oil. This was the incredible woman who had implied that she loved him, or at least that things were headed that direction.

Randi slipped her arms around him and whispered in his ear. "Whatever that thought is, save it for later. We've got to get away from that Zam bad guy."

"Zambada." He stepped back and took her hand. "And he *is* a bad guy. A mean, crazy dude." He handed her his shoes then turned and waded into the bone-chilling water of an arriving wave. Matt gasped from the shock to his nervous system.

Still hidden from anyone on Second Beach, he took a deep breath, gritted his teeth, and dove ahead into the water. The piercing cold stung his face and gripped his body. It stole his breath, squeezing him like a vice. Matt fought the urge to surface as he swam with an underwater breast stroke toward the rock.

The cold saltwater stung his eyes, but a few strokes later, the shadowy form of the rock came into view. He grasped the edges, pulled his head up on the south side, and peered around it to the north. Matt scanned the beach several times and saw no one, nothing mysterious or threatening.

The cold had already penetrated to the core of his body and, in a few seconds, the shivering began. He motioned Randi around the point, pushed off the rock, and swam toward the sandy beach.

Randi beat him to the sand.

He waved her on.

She ran to the bushes at the base of the cliff, slipped behind one of them, and waited.

Matt scampered across the sand to join her. "I didn't see any signs of him.'

"Me, neither," Randi whispered. "Here are your shoes." She stepped from the bushes. "It's my turn to lead."

"That wasn't part of the plan."

"When there's danger or whatever, we need to share it."

"But I drug you into this. You shouldn't even *be* in danger."

"We talked about that already. It's a dead issue. Matt, I told you where I wanted to be right now. And you need to let me lead."

Her words fit several more pieces into the puzzle of Randi Richards. She was strong and became even stronger in tense situations that threatened her physically. But in relationally tense situations, she fell apart. Probably due to her parents. Maybe he could help her with that, if he didn't hurt her in the process.

She raised her eyebrows.

"Go, Ran. I'm right behind you."

In another ten seconds, they stopped near the base of a forty-foot-high cliff at the edge of bushes lining a small creek bed. Though early in the season, the small creek, which usually cascaded down the dirt cliff, had already gone dry. Not having to deal with water would make their climb easier.

The climb should have taken only five minutes, but they stopped to check the beach whenever bare spots in the vegetation threatened to expose them. Being caught while climbing the cliff would get them killed.

Fifteen minutes after they had begun the run up the beach, Matt and Randi had climbed the cliff and now crouched behind a bush at the edge of the forest.

Matt peered through the foliage. "If we stay a hundred yards to this side of the trail, we should be able to hide while we work our way back to the trail head."

Though it was only a mile and a half, the cautious trek through the trees took them more than forty-five minutes. When they reached the top of the hill above the parking area, Matt led Randi to an observation point seventy-five yards from the trail. "I can only see the western edge of the parking area. My truck is there, but I can't see the spot where the Hummer was parked."

Randi pointed to their left. "Let's move along the ridge. If it's there, we'll spot it. And if we don't see the Hummer, we'd better take advantage of that and get out of Dodge."

"Maybe."

After moving ahead for a few moments, Randi tugged on his shirt. She pointed at another opening between the trees toward the spot where the Hummer had been parked. "Looks like he's gone."

"Let's move down to my truck. But, Ran, we need to be careful. This guy is notorious for setting traps, deadly ones."

Chapter 8

"Where do you suppose Zambada went?" Randi gave him a squinty-eyed frown.

Matt had seen that look enough today to know it meant she wouldn't be satisfied until she got an answer.

He peered over Randi's shoulder from their concealed location in the trees. "He's somewhere in the vicinity—you can be sure of that—and still looking for us."

Her eyes widened. "The Third Beach trail head. He could be parked there to see if we jumped between the two trails to bypass him."

Randi's suggestion troubled him. They were hidden in the trees no more than thirty yards from his truck. But the Third Beach trail head was only a half mile down the road. If Zambada were there ... "Ran, if you're right, he could start the Hummer and drive in here with almost no warning. Let's move closer to the truck. I'll need you to watch for Zambo while I check out my truck."

"Can't we just jump in and head for Forks?"

"This guy wouldn't leave a perfectly good truck for us to escape in. Remember, his plan is to knock us off."

"You think he's hiding nearby, using your truck to lure us?"

"The truck is bait even if Zambo isn't here. I'm thinking the truck is either dead in the water or rigged with a bomb."

Randi cupped his cheeks and her eyes widened. "If there's any chance of a bomb, Matt, I don't want you anywhere near that truck. I mean it." She grabbed a hand full of his shirt. "I ... I won't let you go. I'd rather cut cross country on foot to Quillayute. There's a phone at the weather station. We can call for help."

"Didn't you say he came by there looking for me? He saw us together, so I'm guessing he'll check the weather station. He might have rigged the station too?"

The fear in Randi's wide hazel eyes cut into Matt's heart. But he couldn't let her pain stop him. Randi had no understanding of a man like Zambada. "I know a little about Zambada and about bombs. Before I bailed on the cartel, they made me attend a one-day course in, for lack of a better term, narco-terrorism. My instructor was the great Zambo. Let me check out the truck. I won't get in it yet, I promise."

"So now you're a narco-terrorist? Did they give you an AK-47?"

"They would have if I'd stayed."

She released his shirt. "Have you ever killed anyone, Matt?" Her eyes and face looked weird. Not angry, just freaked out.

"No, I've never killed anyone." He dropped his gaze to the ground. "Even though I didn't deal for long, I can't say that for certain about the drugs I sold. They might have killed people by degrees, or by overdose."

Randi put a hand on his shoulder. "I didn't really think those things about you. You know, you're going to have to deal with all that guilt one of these days, but now isn't the time. Sorry I asked."

"Time to change the subject. Let's move closer, but I need you to keep watch."

He left Randi in the trees twenty yards from his truck. She was positioned in a shallow ravine ten feet below the level of the parking area, where she had visibility up the road toward the Third Beach trail.

Matt scrambled to the bank below his parking spot and looked up at the underside of his truck. "Well, well, well. Zambo left me a gift. Wrapped it too, in duct tape."

"What?" Randi whispered loudly from behind him.

"There's a bomb stuck on the underside of my truck with a magnet."

"Matt, don't you dare—" She gasped when he crawled up the bank toward his truck.

He turned toward her. "This has Zambo's trademark on it. Wrapped in tape to hide what's inside. Probably Tovex and a mercury-tilt detonation device."

"Matt, please don't go near it."

But he had to. Feeling it was the only way to verify its construction. Then he would back away. "Randi, don't freak out on me. What I'm doing is safe. If we try to drive away in the truck or jump around in the bed, that's another story."

Before he could climb up the slope to the parking area, Randi was at his side. "Wait. Are you absolutely sure you need to do this?"

"It's the only way we can get my truck back. I have to check it out before I disarm it."

"Disarm a car bomb?" Randi's voice rose in pitch and volume. "Even the police don't do that. They send in robots, or just blow up the whole thing."

"Please, Ran. Go back to that big spruce tree where I asked you to wait. Watch for our friend while I check out his little present. I promise not to open it. I'm only going to touch it. That won't set it off."

She jerked his head toward her, shaking hers. "So help me, Matt, you'd better be careful."

"I will." And he would be careful, because, for the first time in months, he really did want a future.

After Randi reached the spruce tree, he crawled up the bank and slid under his truck. Matt ran his fingertips lightly over the tape-encased bomb.

Bumps marked the spots where the cartridges of Tovex had been positioned. By process of elimination, Matt determined the location of the switch.

What he was going to attempt could work, in theory. He had a better than fifty-percent chance of disarming this insidious device. But Randi might come unglued when she realized what he was doing. She'd get over it and, with a little luck, they would get away in his truck. But first he had to convince her he was the deliverer who could save them from the cartel's version of hell.

He slid down the bank and scampered back to her side.

The stress lines etched in her face told him everything. He didn't need her words, but he got them anyway.

"Matt Mathison, don't ever do that to me again. When you touched that bomb—"

He pressed his fingers over her lips. "I was as safe then as I am now touching your lips. Although your lips are much nicer."

"How can you joke about something that dangerous?"

Whether she knew it or not, her question was loaded. He could touch the bomb, but he wouldn't touch her question. "Here's what needs to happen."

She glared at him but remained silent.

"We can't waste any more time. Zambo could drive in any second. And I don't want you freaking out at some critical point. So please, listen until I'm done, then I'll open it up for comments." He put his hands on her shoulders. "I'm going to open the passenger-side door of the truck and get my gun."

Her eyes widened. She put her hand on his arm and squeezed.

"The bomb won't go off. You can even shoot the Tovex explosive and it won't detonate. But if the switch gets tilted, a drop of mercury runs to the other end, closing the circuit, and my truck is history, stereo and all."

"You're joking about it again."

"Sorry."

She frowned and tightened her grip on his arm.

"I'll hide behind that rock near the base of the bank. It's about forty feet from the truck, but I can see the bomb from down there. Then I shoot the bomb and it—"

"It blows you and your truck to kingdom come." She grabbed Matt and squeezed him in a bear hug, surprising him with her strength. "Don't do it, please."

He pried her arms loose. "Randi, the bomb won't explode. But even if it does, there's probably less than one chance in several thousand that some piece of shrapnel can hit the tiny part of me that will be exposed."

"But that tiny part is your head, Matt. This is crazy. Let's start running for Quillayute now."

"I'll be fine. I wouldn't risk losing you by doing something stupid."

The look in her eyes said he'd gotten her attention.

"You'll be tucked away behind the spruce with five feet of solid wood to protect you. The bullet will destroy the detonation mechanism before the mercury can run down. If by some freak circumstance the circuit gets closed when things fly apart, my truck is history. Then we'll go to your Plan B. But this is going to work. I know it."

"You're crazy. And I'm insane for listening."

"Ran, if I'm crazy, it's like a fox. You'll see. Now wait here. But after you hear my shot, if I motion for you to come, run for the truck. We'll need to get away immediately. If Zambo's in the area, he'll hear the shot and in about ten seconds he'll figure out what I'm up to."

"Matt, I hope this isn't what life with you is going to be like for the next fifty years."

So they were trying to escape an assassin, and Randi was planning their future? "Regardless, for me this is safer than football." He smiled.

She didn't.

"Stay completely behind the tree until you hear my shot. You need to pray this works." He touched her cheek, then slipped away.

The sound of a vehicle echoed through the trees.

Matt stooped low, hugging the grill of his truck, and waited.

A pickup, coming from La Push.

After it passed the parking area, he moved to the passenger-side door. Matt opened the door, lifted the console cover, and unlocked his gun safe. After pulling out his .38 Super, he closed the door and slid down the bank, where he crouched behind the three-foot-high rock.

Even when exposing just the top of his head, from this distance, it was an easy shot to hit the bomb. And his shot shouldn't damage his truck, unless the bomb exploded.

Matt looked toward the large spruce tree.

Randi had ducked out of sight behind its big trunk.

He shot a short prayer heavenward, took careful aim, putting the laser beam on the right side of the bomb, and squeezed the trigger.

Chapter 9

Matt ducked behind the rock while the loud report of his .38 rang in his ears.

No explosion. The only noise that followed was the echo of the gunshot from the trees.

Either his scheme had worked, or he had missed the bomb completely.

He raised his head and studied the underside of his truck.

The bomb was gone.

Matt scurried up the bank and looked on the far side of the truck. Remnants of the explosive device lay scattered across the dirt parking lot. The bullet had obliterated the fuse assembly, but the two Tovex cartridges remained bound together by the duct tape.

He scooped up the cartridges, ran down the bank, and hid them under the rock he'd used for cover.

The police could pick them up later.

Randi stood beside the spruce tree, twisting auburn curls with her fingers and watching him.

He motioned for her to come, then turned and scrambled up the bank to his truck. Before jumping in, he opened the cylinder of his gun and checked for ammo. He was out.

Maybe it was a good thing he didn't know that before he made the shot. But now, if Zambada showed up, they had no weapon.

Matt slid into his seat.

Randi pulled open the passenger's door and slipped in beside him. "You're sure the truck is good to go?"

"Yeah." He fired up the engine. "I don't know if it was luck, skill, or the prayer, but my shot destroyed the detonation mechanism. I hid the explosives under that rock I used for cover."

"Let's get out of here before something else happens and I wet my pants."

Matt did a backward U-turn until his truck faced the road. "At least your date with me wasn't boring."

"Hardly." Randi grabbed his arm. "Wait—something's coming on the road, but I can't see it through the trees."

"I'm not gonna pull out of here until I know it's not Zambo. He would gun us down while we pass by him. He's done it to others who've tried."

"What about your gun?"

"All out of ammo."

"Great!" She exhaled a blast of air.

"That car's on your side. Tell me when you can see—"

"It's a dark-colored Hummer."

He jammed the gas pedal to the floor.

Dirt, gravel, and dust exploded from the wheels of his truck. The big pickup fishtailed until the wheels caught pavement.

Matt yanked the wheel to his left.

They rocketed onto the road.

Powered by a big V-8 engine, the truck burned rubber as they accelerated toward La Push.

With a sharp turn ahead, he couldn't take his eyes off the road. "How close is he?"

The truck slid into the turn.

Halfway in, he hit the gas and fought for control as they exited the turn with the wheels spinning.

"He's more than a hundred yards behind us now. You opened up our lead."

The road straightened. He glanced at Randi.

She stared back at him, eyes intense and questioning. "Ran, what is it?"

"I drove into La Push once. The road dead ends there."

"I know. But it's not like I had a choice."

Chapter 10

Matt hit the brake hard as they passed a motel and a store at the edge of the village. Accidentally running over a school kid would be a lot worse than the death Zambada had planned for them.

The businesses would have phones, but they had to shake Zambada first. If Matt stopped, neither he nor Randi would be alive to place a call.

Randi twisted in her seat and looked behind. "You slowed and now he's gaining on us."

They flew by a cross street. "If there's another cross street, maybe we can play Ring-Around-the-Block until we can get out of town."

"He's slowing, Matt, but still following.

"Hang on." He yanked the wheel to the right.

They slid sideways onto the second cross street.

Matt accelerated between weather-beaten buildings to the next corner. "Here we go again, Ran. We need to get out of the village before he hems us in."

With the truck wheels spinning, Matt accelerated out of the turn.

They sailed by the marina on their left.

"I can't see him now."

He rounded the next corner and sped back toward the main street. "Time to watch ahead of us, Ran, in case he doubled back."

"Yeah. I'll take the right. You watch the left."

"Hang on again." He steered hard left onto the main drag, headed out of town.

"Behind us, Matt. A block down. He's turning around, but…"

Matt shoved the accelerator to the floor. "But what?"

They shot out of the east end of the village, passing the store and motel.

She put a hand on his shoulder. "There were SUVs all over the village, even another Hummer"

"What are you trying to tell me?"

"I'm not sure, but I don't think that was Zambada's Hummer. With the sun shining back onto it, it looked dark purple. When we first saw it, the Hummer was only a silhouette against the sunlight."

"Great. We can't stop now in case that's him behind us. But if it's not Zambada back there..." Matt drove up the hill and passed the Beach 2 trail head, trying to solve the equation in his head, the one that could save their lives. There were too many unknowns and the one thing he did know frightened him. "If he didn't go to the village, there's only one place he can be sure to catch us..."

After a few seconds Randi squeezed his shoulder. "When do you plan to tell me where this one place is? Or do I have to wait until I hear him shooting?" She stared down the road ahead of them. "The intersection of Quillayute and La Push Roads. That's where he'll be waiting, isn't it?"

Matt steered through a winding stretch of road lined with evergreens. "It has to be the place. Either way we go, we pass through that intersection. I didn't detonate the bomb. Zambo didn't hear it explode, so he'll assume we did the impossible, resurrected my truck, and then headed to Forks for help."

The trees they were passing turned from evergreens to deciduous trees. The river and a bridge lay a short distance ahead.

"You *did* do the impossible. Scared the living daylights out of me, but you did it."

"We'll have to run Zambo's gauntlet to get cell reception unless—my landlord has a phone in her house on Mora Road. No. She's a widow lady. I don't want to risk bringing Zambo to her doorstep. Got any ideas?"

They crossed the bridge and approached the Mora Road intersection.

"The weather station. It's got a landline phone. That's Mora Road coming up. Turn down it and catch the end of Quillayute Road above the campground. I drive that way sometimes when I run. We can avoid Zambada for now. He'll be waiting beyond the airport, at the other end of Quillayute Road to watch the road to Forks."

"I knew there must be some reason I ran into a meteorologist. She's not just a cute weathercaster on local TV either."

"I'm not sure how to take that. But after we get out of here, you can tell me what you meant, as long as you leave my hair out of it."

He turned onto Mora Road. "But your hair is a part of the package, a very nice package, unlike the one Zambo gave me."

"There's an old hangar beside the weather station. Pilots who fly in sometimes park their planes in it. You can hide your truck there while we use the phone. You need to go up the hill to where the road turns to the right. The gate to the weather station is—"

"Ran, I picked you up there this morning, remember?"

"Oh, yeah. With intentions of dumping me." She shot him a glance and a coy look he hadn't seen before.

"What can I say? I was an idiot." An idiot who didn't want to endanger Randi. But he had, so he was worse than an idiot. "He's linked you and me and he's linked you and the weather station. We'll need to be careful at the weather station. He might have left another gift for us."

A mile down Mora Road, Matt turned onto Quillayute Road, heading toward the old airport.

A blue sedan, backed up against a barricade, sat on the turn-in to a closed timber access road.

An uneasy feeling grew into a knot in Matt's stomach as he drove by the vehicle.

"There were three men in that car." Randi pointed a thumb at her window.

He slapped the steering wheel with one hand. "I think Zambada called for reinforcements. Did the sedan pull out?"

"Not yet, but the turn by the airport is just ahead. I'm going to lose sight of them."

He slowed for the coming sharp turn in the road. "We can't risk turning in at the weather station. They could trap us there and gun us down. I think we'd better—"

Randi gasped. "The blue car just flew out of the corner."

"Great! They're chasing us straight to where Zambada is waiting." He shoved the gas pedal to the floor.

"Zambada could be waiting at the intersection or hiding anywhere along La Push Road this side of 101. Matt, what are we going to do?"

He braked for a curve. "Let me think for a second. You pray. I'll drive."

"I'll pray with my eyes open, if you don't mind."

"Then please watch that blue sedan while you pray." Matt glanced her way.

Randi's eyes widened while her lips formed the letter, O. "We have a way out of here, Matt. We can outrun this guy on foot. We could outrun all of them. We can run through the woods ... all the way to Forks if we have to." Randi gasped again. "They're coming right up behind us."

"Let me know the second any guns poke out. I'll have to take drastic measures."

"Like what?"

"Do you really want me to freak you out?"

"No. You did that the first time I met you."

"Because I thought you were Zambada."

She shot him a wide-eyed glance. "You mistook me for him? And I'm supposed to trust *you* with drastic measures."

"You wanna to trade places?"

She didn't reply.

He glanced in the side mirror.

The sedan was closing on them.

"Matt, they're trying to pass us!"

He swerved in front of the blue sedan, cutting it off, then drove down the centerline.

Randi's finger in front of his nose pointed out the driver's window. "That's the driveway for the bed and breakfast. We're almost to the intersection."

The road curved left about fifty yards from the intersection with La Push Road. The curve, framed by half-grown trees, rushed at them.

"Guns! On both sides!"

"Ahead of us too, Ran. The Hummer's parked at the intersection. Zambo has his gun. They've got us in a crossfire."

Chapter 11

"Matt, why aren't they shooting at us?"

He glanced at Randi.

Wide eyes stared back at him.

"Because they'd be shooting at each other." But when they entered the turn, the shooting angle would change.

Straight ahead, Zambada stood beside his Hummer on the left side of the road.

The blue sedan bore down on them from behind.

Quillayute Road angled to the right a few yards in front of them.

In three or four seconds, Matt's truck would enter the turn, giving the shooters a safe, firing angle. How could he prevent it? Only one thought came to mind.

"Get down, Randi. Brace yourself between the dashboard and the seat."

She leaned down and placed both hands on the dash.

They entered the turn.

Matt jerked the wheel to the left and accelerated directly at Zambada.

No shots. His maneuver had left the gunmen still shooting directly at each other. That would not change until Matt steered back to the right. He crossed the centerline, bearing down on his target.

Zambada dove to his right to avoid being mashed between the two vehicles.

A few feet from the Hummer, Matt jerked the wheel hard right. His truck dealt the Hummer a glancing blow, caroming off the Hummer and back toward the intersection.

Matt hit the brakes.

They slid into the intersection.

A logging truck on La Push Road swerved to miss them. It flew by with its air horn blaring the truckdriver's complaint.

Matt jerked the wheel hard left and shoved the gas pedal to the floor.

With the rear wheels spinning and black smoke billowing from the tires, they fishtailed down La Push Road headed toward Forks.

The popping of an assault rifle sent a spray of bullets at them.

Matt ducked and pushed Randi's head onto the seat.

Three loud whacks sounded from the back of the cab.

As the truck accelerated, Matt glanced into his rearview mirror.

The sedan spun out, destroying the aim of the two gunmen. It slid to a stop, then accelerated up La Push Road in pursuit.

"Are you okay, Matt?" Randi sat up and put her hand on his shoulder.

"Yeah. Both me and the truck. Otherwise ..."

"Let's not think about that. Just get us to Forks."

The speedometer passed eighty miles-per-hour on the narrow, tree-lined road.

He steered safely through one turn and sped down the next straight stretch.

The logging truck turned onto a timber-access road, clearing the road ahead of them.

But the sedan closed, rapidly.

"I can't outrun them all the way to Forks. But at least Zambo's temporarily out of the equation."

"Did you hit him? I just closed my eyes and prayed."

"He dropped his gun and jumped out of the way. And the guys in the sedan didn't get any good shots either. Their driver had a little trouble following us." He paused and shot her a glance. "Somebody must have answered your prayer."

"No. He didn't. I asked Him to get us to heaven with no pain along the way."

Matt's laugh was a little short on mirth. "Don't give up our life on earth yet."

"But the sedan is gaining on us."

"He's probably got several hundred horses under the hood of that car."

"Can we go any faster?"

He glanced out the side window at the blur of vegetation passing by them. "We hit ninety on the last straight stretch." He braked and steered left. "My truck needs to slow in the turns more than their car."

The tires screeched.

"Hang on!"

His truck spun out halfway through the turn.

Matt over steered to the right, then to the left.

He brought the truck nearly to a stop to regain control and then punched the gas pedal. They rocketed ahead again.

"Doggone it! I lost our lead. They'll be on us in a few seconds."

"Matt ... how much do love this truck?"

He squinted as he glanced back at Randi's wide hazel eyes. "There's someone beside me I care about a lot more than this truck."

"Matt Mathison. You picked a fine time to say something like that. But back to your truck."

"It's my baby, but can't you think of a more appropriate question? These guys are about to start shooting." Matt accelerated down a short straightaway.

"Then it *is* an appropriate question. Listen. When you leave that sharp turn ahead, shift down to low range. But don't use your brakes, don't show any brake lights. They won't know you're slowing down."

"Ran, that's hard on the transmission."

"Not as hard as their bullets would be on us."

"One of them just stuck a gun barrel out the window."

"Shift down as you exit. When we accelerate out of the turn, hit your brakes. Do a panic stop."

"But they'll rear end—"

"Yeah. Really hard. Just do it, Matt!"

Matt's right hand grabbed the gearshift lever on the console. "This could cause whiplash. Put your head against your head rest. Here we go." He jammed the transmission into low.

The truck decelerated.

The sedan ran up to their rear bumper.

Two guns jutted out opposite windows.

Matt stomped hard on the brake pedal.

Chapter 12

The big sedan slammed into the rear of Matt's truck.

The whump of crumpling metal sounded.

The impact drove him back into the seat with the force of an unimpeded, three-hundred-pound defensive lineman.

Both vehicles stopped in the roadway.

For a moment it was silent, except for the hissing noise coming in through Matt's opened window.

He shook off his stunned feeling and glanced at Randi. "You alright?"

"I think so. Get us out of here. Now."

Matt glanced in his rearview mirror.

Smoke or steam billowed from the front of the big sedan. Airbags, like large balloons, filled the front seats. But they were deflating now.

Matt mashed the accelerator to the floor and prayed his truck could still roll. The squealing of tires and the smell of burnt rubber brought a weak smile to his face. His truck could more than just roll. It left a trail of black smoke as the tires fought for traction on the blacktop.

Randi twisted to look behind them. "I'll watch our back side. You get us to Forks."

He accelerated to seventy miles-per-hour, trying to put as much distance between them and the gunmen as possible.

Randi swung her head back toward him. "The sedan won't be coming after us. Not in time to catch up."

"But the Hummer still worries me."

"I'll watch for it."

"We could have cell phone reception in about a mile or so." He rounded a corner and accelerated into a straight stretch of road. "My cell phone is beside the gun safe in the console. Call 911 as soon as some bars show up."

Randi pulled out the phone and flipped it open, surveying its display and assortment of buttons.

"Just push the dialer icon at the bottom."

"I will. As soon as we have a signal." She put her thumb over the button. "Any ideas about how we tell a ten-second version of our story to the call operator?"

"We need to get the right people involved from the get-go. This is going to take more than just the Forks Police." Matt shook his head as he sought appropriate words. "Tell them we've been attacked by people with assault rifles, and we know they have ties to a Mexican drug cartel."

"Coming out of the blue, it's going to sound pretty far-fetched to the operator."

"Doesn't matter. If we stick to our story, and emphasize the guns and the danger, they have no choice but to respond."

"We've got bars now."

While she spoke to the operator, Randi's face looked as intense as when she had looked up at him from that mud hole. After she had told their story, and repeated it twice, she relaxed and closed his cell.

"What are you doing? You have to stay on the line until we have help."

"They didn't terminate the call. We lost the connection. But they're dispatching two patrol cars to La Push Road and Highway 101. The dispatcher said we might see a Deputy Sheriff's car there too."

"That's only two or three minutes away and no one is following that I can see."

She touched his arm lightly. "What do we tell them about us? The question will come up at some point."

"They'll probably take me to jail right away, Ran."

"If we have a choice, I don't want them to separate us, Matt. I'll tell them I was helping a drug dealer. It's the truth."

"No, Ran. I'm not a dealer now. You won't lie and you can't come with me to jail."

Even best case, the probing questions would eventually be asked. Either the police or a lawyer would ask them, and Randi could never forgive him if she knew all the dirty details of his former life. It had only been a short life, but it wasn't pretty.

Matt blew out a blast of air. "If only I hadn't—if I could just erase some of what I've done."

"You've completely changed the direction of your life. Let the guilt go, Matt. It's still controlling you. There's no reason that I can't stand with you through—"

He pounded the steering wheel. "You don't understand, Randi. And if you did, you wouldn't want—"

"Yes, I would. You're being a pigheaded fool, Matt Mathison. I know what you're thinking. You explain theology to me, what you profess to believe, then you behave as if you believe something entirely different." She shook her head until auburn waves of hair flew. "You—"

"It's not that simple. There are consequences to—"

"But it *is* that simple. You're forgiven, Matt. Go and sin no more. After two thousand years, that's still His command, and it's the only advice He has for you. When we start talking to the police, you're going to have some really difficult decisions to make. Make them in light of being forgiven, in light of the fact that you're going to do what's right from this point forward. Tell them the truth, but don't shut me out."

She caught his gaze and her voice broke. "I'm in danger just like you are. Like you said, we'll both need protection of some sort. Don't isolate me, Matt. Let me in ... with you."

The pleading look in her watery eyes ripped at his heart. This woman was genuine through and through. Beauty radiated from every part of Randi, body, mind, and spirit. She was a fountain of joy and had the heart of a champion. Why couldn't he simply do what she asked? To let her remain a part of his life no matter what the justice system decided?

Matt's answer came from that part of his heart and mind where guilt ruled. The place where Satan still punched the buttons to bring him down to what he was, a vile man, a hypocritical nothing, a spiritual zero rubbed out.

Two words sounded repeatedly in his mind … unworthy and unforgiven. He didn't deserve her, and she didn't deserve someone like him.

Reasons why he couldn't accept Randi's invitation rolled across his mind like storm surge waves. Besides not deserving her, spending more time with her could still get her killed. He wouldn't put her in any more danger.

Finally, he doubted she would want a relationship with him after details of his past were brought out by the police, or by an attorney, if there was a trial.

She didn't understand the depths to which he had sunk. A clever lawyer would put him on the stand and make him look like scum in her eyes.

Hurting Randi now was far better than destroying her later. He looked into her eyes and scanned her face.

Hurting her now would kill him.

She looked at him, and her eyes overflowed. "Matt, what you told me on the beach wasn't true. After hearing what I wanted, if you cared for me like you said, you would want me with you through whatever lies ahead." Randi wiped the tears away without breaking eye contact. She was obviously reading his expression, maybe his mind. She held his gaze for a moment longer, but when he didn't reply, she shook her head and looked away as tears spilled from her eyes and streamed down her cheeks.

Two police cars sat by the Smokehouse Restaurant at the intersection with Highway 101.

Matt turned in to park beside them.

Without a single word, or perhaps because of his lack of words, he had lost Randi Richards. And along with her, he'd lost his last chance of injecting any meaning into his miserable existence.

Chapter 13

Randi studied Matt's face, seeking some kind of explanation for why he would go back on his word to never abandon her.

But Matt offered none. He parked beside the patrol cars near the Smokehouse Restaurant and got out as if she didn't exist. Matt was going to walk away and leave her alone to face the whatever danger lay ahead for her.

She had handed her heart to him, and he hadn't wanted it enough to reply.

Twice today he said he cared for her and then proved he didn't. The rejection was complete, total, and less understandable than her parent's rejection after she told them she'd embraced Christianity.

Randi partially understood their reaction. After all, with her parents, it was a war of worldviews, atheism versus theism. But she and Matt shared a common worldview, the way, the truth, and the life—Jesus—and still he turned his back on her.

As she had said, tears made a lousy lullaby. A lullaby she would sing tonight, and it would not bring sleep, only the incapacitating ache of a shattered heart.

As Randi slid out of Matt's truck and crunched through the gravel to meet the two policemen, the other reality wedged its way into her conscious mind. These policemen's protection was her only hope of staying alive once Zambada resumed his hunt for them.

Staying alive ... sometimes it didn't seem worth the effort and certainly not the heartache.

* * *

"Matt Mathison?" The taller of the two policemen called out before Matt drew near them.

"Yes." He turned toward Randi. "And Randi Richards."

"I'm Officer Lomax. We didn't see anyone following you. Where are the people with the guns?"

"Thanks to Randi, we found a way to keep them occupied while we drove here to meet you." He motioned toward her.

Randi stepped beside him. "There were two vehicles. Matt did some creative driving and stopped them both ... temporarily." She had taken out the pony tail. Her hair hung in waves around her shoulders. Even with all they'd been through she would catch any man's eye.

Lomax's gaze scanned Randi a little longer than Matt thought necessary.

Matt squelched the biting remark that almost slipped out. He could make no claim on her. Earlier in the day maybe, but certainly not now.

His jealousy morphed to loneliness and dread, loneliness from losing Randi, dread because of the uncertain future he faced, a future with frightening possibilities.

"The call center operator said you mentioned automatic weapons."

Matt nodded. "I think they were AK-47s."

The officer's eyebrows rose. "And you're still alive?"

"Come here, Officer Lomax." Matt whirled, jogged toward the back of his truck, and pointed to the holes in the cab.

"Take a look at this, Jim." Lomax stepped toward the cab and ran his fingers over three bullet holes.

The other trooper, Jim, muttered a mild expletive as he surveyed the holes.

Lomax turned back to Matt. "Who did you say these people were? Drug dealers?"

That was putting it mildly. "They're not your run-of-the-mill drug dealers. They're part of the Tijuana Cartel,

Arellano's gang. One of them is his preferred hit man, an assassin called Zambada."

Lomax shook his head. "If you're right, they're certainly out of their territory. And we're nearly 200 miles from the I-5 corridor."

"They're here because they wanted to kill me before I could do what I'm doing right now."

"What happened to your arm?" Lomax pointed at his wounded triceps.

"Zambada nicked me when we dove behind a log. It's not deep. I'm okay."

"Jim, call for an EMT. His arm needs attention." Lomax took another close look at his wound. "It doesn't look very deep, but you don't want that to get infected."

"These guys could show here and, if they have a mind to take you on, you wouldn't stand a chance with your hand guns. Can you have someone check me out at the police station? Someplace safer than here?"

Lomax tapped Jim's shoulder.

Jim aborted the call he was making.

"Have Kent meet us at the station in a few minutes." Lomax turned back to Matt. "Let's at least get descriptions of the vehicles and the suspects so we can alert everyone."

Lomax took descriptions of Zambada, the blue sedan, and Zambada's black Hummer, then radioed them in. When a state policeman showed up, Lomax asked him to check out the intersection where the last shooting and the collision occurred, a place in the county, outside Forks Police's jurisdiction.

Randi kept glancing down La Push Road.

Thinking about what might appear racing down that road toward them brought a nauseating knot to Matt's gut. Standing here in the middle of a parking area with only three officers armed with handguns for protection wasn't safe. But it looked like Lomax was nearly done.

"I think we need to get you two out of the open and down to the police station." Lomax said.

Jim nodded. "Then we need to turn this over to the chief."

Lomax met Jim's gaze. "This is organized crime we're dealing with, and we've only got a five-man force. He'll call in the feds."

Matt sighed in relief. Maybe this would play out as he had hoped. With the FBI involved, his odds of a decent future improved. But Randi's future troubled him. She could be forced into a protection program. Whether the protection was short-term or long-term, meeting him had disrupted her life in a huge way. It was one more thing that told him she was better off without Matt Mathison around.

But what about Matt Mathison without Randi?

Matt was still wrestling with that question when another patrol car pulled in.

Officer Lomax had a short conversation with the driver, then returned to Matt and Randi. "Officer Braithwaite will bring your truck. We'll need to do some forensics on it. I'll take you to the station now."

During the ride to the police station Randi sat by his side in the back of the patrol car. She stared out the window in silence until patrol the car turned from East Division Street into the parking lot for Forks City Hall, which housed the police station.

When the car stopped beside the large, light-gray building, Randi looked at him, opened her mouth, then closed it.

What was there left to say? She'd probably said it all twenty minutes ago.

Twenty-five minutes, a few bandages and a shot with a hypodermic needle later, Matt and Randi sat side-by-side in a small room inside the Forks police station. The chief had joined Lomax, and there were more questions, quite a few for Matt and some for Randi. Then there were questions about Matt and Randi.

Randi's obvious discomfort and her curt answers shortened the probes into their relationship.

But Matt's answers about the cartel began to draw a picture of his involvement with the organization.

After Matt mentioned the offer to join their operation, the chief's questions stopped.

He studied Matt for a moment, then bent over the desk and looked Matt straight in the eye. "Young man, I'm not planning to arrest you, nevertheless you don't have to answer our questions if you don't want to, and you can call for an attorney."

Matt held the gaze of this kind-faced man with a booming, authoritative voice. "I know that, sir, but I want to answer your questions. However, I think it will take the FBI to act on my answers. The resurrected Tijuana Cartel is a powerful organization headed by a man named Arellano. I know enough about the operation to hurt them. If any of them are caught, I know enough to convict them on several charges."

The chief looked from Matt to Randi. "That's why I've already called the FBI field office in Seattle. An agent is on a helicopter headed our way."

"In the meantime, what about Randi and me?"

The chief 's gaze darted between them. "The meantime won't be much time. Special Agent Peterson will be here in another thirty minutes. I've got officers standing guard outside. We have backup from the county sheriff and the state police. You'll be safe until Peterson arrives. He's a good agent. Lots of experience. He'll know how to deal with the crew you two have been up against."

A measure of peace washed over Matt. The first he'd felt since he confessed his feelings for Randi in the cove. But the peace was short lived. Agent Peterson would probe more deeply with his questions than the chief had done. What would Randi think about some of his answers? Did she even care at this point?

The next few hours could prove to be an ordeal, one that might change his life forever. Could Matt make it through this without Randi? A deeper question quickly replaced the original one. Did he even *want* to make it through this without her?

Matt looked at Randi.

She looked up at him, her expression empty, haunted.

Her face said it all. His questions were moot.

Chapter 14

The *wop, wop* of a helicopter rotor grew louder.

Matt walked to the window as a dark gray chopper hovered over a grassy area by the police station. It slowly came to rest, and the engine whined its relief as the rotor spun down.

He looked across the room at Randi. Her haunted expression had morphed to something worse.

She sat in a chair twisting her long, auburn hair around her fingers and staring at the wall as if it were a theater screen showing some horror movie.

Matt needed to help her. "Do you feel like a helicopter ride, Ran?"

"No, thanks. I think I'll pass."

"The thing is, we probably don't have that option." He glanced outside. "Here come the FBI agents. We'll get a lot more questions, I'm sure. But maybe some answers about our future." He remained by the window, watching as a seemingly endless stream of concerns for himself and Randi flowed through his mind.

Her voice came from behind him. "We need some answers, Matt. I need to know about my job. The Quillayute sounding will be missing if I can't launch the radiosonde this afternoon. That sounding is an important input to the numerical progs. I need to call my boss in Port Angeles to let him know about our ... well, to let him know something."

If only a phone call could take care of his problems. Depending on the thinking of the FBI agent who just climbed out of the chopper, he could be separated from Randi, put in jail, and treated like the criminal that he was. "Matt ..."

He turned away from the window toward Randi. The fear displayed in her wide eyes reeled him in like a spent fish, pulling him across the room to her. "You're not doing well, are you?"

Her head bent forward, fingers rubbing her forehead. "So many changes, all out of my control." Randi's hand waved in protest. "Restrictions, protection. I'm worried and a little frightened, I guess."

"It's going to turn out all right." It probably wasn't a wise thing to do, but he put a hand on her shoulder.

She relaxed.

"Whatever happens, I'll protect you." If that was humanly possible. He prayed that, somehow, he'd be close enough to comfort her, assure her. But maybe his presence would produce the opposite effect.

"Like you did this morning?" She placed a hand on his arm, slid it down and took his hand.

Her reaction surprised him. "I thought we made a pretty good team this morning. Zambada is a professional killer, and he had three good swings at us, but he struck out. Now he's the one on the run."

"Yeah, I guess we—"

"Excuse me." A deep voice boomed across the room. It came from a tall man dressed in a dark suit.

Randi pulled her hand from Matt's and stood beside him. Her tanned face had turned pink.

Though he wanted to, he shouldn't make too much out of what was only a display of thanks from a touching, caring person. But, without realizing he'd done it, his arm had circled Randi's waist.

The tall man gave them a tight-lipped smile. "I see that at least something is going right for you two today."

How he wished the man's assessment was correct, but nothing of consequence had changed between them. Randi tolerated him because she was upset at facing so many changes in one day.

"I'm Special Agent Peterson, FBI."

A second man in a suit, a much younger man, entered the room.

"And this is Special Agent Ruska." Agent Peterson shoved a hand at Matt.

He gave it a firm shake. "Matt Mathison, and this is Randi Richards."

After the introductions, Peterson motioned toward a table with four chairs around it. "Shall we sit? Chief Lewis's briefing raised a lot of questions. I've got several for you two. When I'm done, you'll probably have some for me."

Randi glanced at Matt. Her darting eyes and fingers twisting her auburn curls said she needed him ... even if she didn't want to need him.

After she sat down, Matt scooted his chair close to hers and sat.

The wild look in her eyes softened as if she were saying thank you.

He took her hand under the table hoping she understood that it meant you're welcome.

Randi glanced down at their clasped hands and squeezed his.

Being this close to her after holding her sent his heart into an all-out sprint, and his stomach climbed onto some wild carnival ride. Who was he kidding? Despite their situation and their disagreements, he was still head over heels for this woman.

"Mr. Mathison ... are you still with us?" The corners of Peterson's mouth edged upward.

Had they been talking to him? "Sorry, sir. Today's been a rough day."

"After what the chief and a couple of his men told me, I would have to agree. But I need your cooperation."

Over the next several minutes, Peterson elicited details about each of Zambada's attacks and the car bomb.

"You disarmed a car bomb?" Peterson's brow furled.

"It felt like a tilt-switch mechanism, so I hunkered down behind a rock and shot the switch off."

Agent Ruska turned toward Peterson and mouthed, "That's crazy."

Peterson gave Ruska a frown and a headshake, then looked back at Matt and Randi. "I'm certain you knew that was a gamble. But in your situation, I might have tried the same thing."

Next, Peterson focused on Matt, drawing out pertinent information about the cartel's organization, its operation, and Matt's involvement.

After several questions, a pattern became clear. Peterson initially asked questions for which the FBI probably already knew the answers. He was evaluating Matt as a witness. Then Peterson questioned Matt about details of the cartel's operations, things Peterson probably did not know.

The most important thing was that Peterson was taking Matt seriously and obviously planned to act on his information. All in all, it gave Matt a more optimistic feeling about his future.

Forty-five minutes later, and several pages into Peterson's notepad, the questions stopped.

"I'm going to be frank with you, young man. All we have regarding your alleged crimes is your word. I believe, if you are willing to help us take these guys down, it would be a waste of taxpayer's money to go after you. I want to go after this cartel, to cripple it, or at least drive it out of the country. They've been expanding activity in Washington State for months. And—" Peterson made eye contact with Matt and Randi "—on the flight over I checked with our intelligence organization. Several interesting people associated with the Tijuana Cartel entered the U.S. a few hours ago."

Matt squeezed Randi's hand, a hand she had left in his through the entire questioning session. "It sounds like they're coming after Randi and me with all their resources. Peterson, you've got to protect Randi. She's innocent."

Randi's grip on his hand tightened. "You need to protect *both* of us."

Was Randi changing her mind about him, or was he simply a source of comfort in her uncertain world? If Randi remained in the picture, he needed to know his odds of walking away a free man. "So you aren't going to prosecute me for anything I did?"

Peterson gave him a stern look that faded to something less threatening. "I don't plan to, Matt. It appears the cartel is already trying to do that. You'd already left that life behind. But the final decision rests in the hands of the federal prosecutor. I'm moving ahead with protection for both of you."

"Thank you, sir."

"However, you need to keep telling us every relevant thing you can remember. Cooperate as best you can." When he met Matt's gaze this time, Peterson's eyes softened. They reminded Matt of his father's proud eyes. "I follow football, and I remember your glory days. UW had high hopes for a certain young man who was a strong leader, a man with integrity, and a highly skilled quarterback. You need to get back to being that kind of man."

At Peterson's last words, Randi squeezed his hand.

Matt looked across the table at Peterson. "Thanks, sir. I'll do my best."

"Were you aware that the U.S. State Department and the DEA have offered five million dollars for information leading to Arellano's arrest?"

"What?" Randi's mouth dropped open.

"Arellano has made the big time." Peterson nodded slowly. "Like his counterpart in Sinaloa."

Did money matter? It certainly could help him rebuild his life. It could even be a substitute for the NFL career he would never have. But the real question was could he ever again be the man Peterson referred to?

And what should he make of Randi's actions over the past hour? She was a good person. Probably just wanted the best for him, wanted him to break the ties to his recent past. Beyond that, she might have no interest in him. But some of her actions contradicted that conclusion.

All of the questions and speculating gave him a huge headache. Before asking for some aspirin, he raised one last question. "Peterson, what's next for Randi ... and for me?"

Peterson looked from Matt to Randi. For the first time, Matt thought he saw confusion in Peterson's eyes. "Are you asking us to separate you two?"

Randi's body tensed. She shook her head, causing waves of auburn hair to dance. "No. That wouldn't be a good idea ... I mean ... from my perspective it wouldn't."

Mixed signals. Over the past two or three hours he'd seen two sides of Randi Richards. One wanted to be near him. The other wanted to protect her heart by putting distance between them.

"One thing is clear," Peterson's voice recovered its previous authority. "We need to get you two out of this area and hide you in a safe place. In about thirty minutes, we'll fly to Seattle, where we plan to keep you in a motel until we find a more permanent location."

Randi sat up in her chair gripping Matt's hand with incredible strength. "What about my job? My things?"

"Give us the keys to your vehicles and your houses. Make a list of personal things that you want, and we'll have our people bring them to you tomorrow. We'll supply whatever you need for tonight." The tall FBI agent rose to his feet. "If you need to make any phone calls, clear them with me or Ruska."

"Everything for tonight?" Randi stared at Peterson with wide eyes.

"You said you two waded around that point. I would imagine unsalty clothes are on the list of necessities for tonight."

"Do I have to give some stranger my underwear size?"

Peterson cleared his throat. "I'll have them schedule a short stop at, say Freddy's. You should be able to get anything you need there. I've got to tend to some other issues now. I'll see you on the chopper in a few minutes."

Peterson strode out the door, leaving Matt and Randi alone in the room.

Matt looked down at the hand he'd held for the past hour, then looked up into her eyes. "I am so sorry I got you involved. This is exactly why I wasn't going to run with you this morning."

Randi sighed. "If we just hadn't run the trail this morning, I would be at home and safe. But ..."

"No, Ran. Zambada may have already had you on his radar. He's pretty shrewd. You'd be better off only if you hadn't run into me at all."

She gave him a curious look, as confusing as her enigmatic smile. "It's improbable that we would run the trail the way we did, that I would go into the cove, that we'd do all that with just the right timing. Maybe there was a purpose behind our meeting."

He nodded but didn't have the heart to say he had botched whatever purpose there might have been.

Could God have wanted them to meet, to bond, to—no. That was the stuff of romance novels. It didn't happen in the real world, a world where evil destroys most of what is good, as it had done to his relationship with Randi.

Chapter 15

Over the past hour and a half at the Forks police station, Randi and Matt had been fed, given an update on the search for Zambada and his accomplices, all still on the loose, and Randi had called her boss explaining her predicament, hinting at the uncertainty in her future. It wasn't her fault, but still seemed that she had let them down.

The door to the conference room opened with a click and a creak. Peterson stuck his head in the opened door. "Time to load up. Did you make your phone calls?"

"Yeah," Randi replied.

"Did you both get enough to eat?"

She quickly closed the lid on her unfinished meal and looked up at Peterson. "Yes, thanks. We hadn't eaten since breakfast."

Peterson stepped away from the conference room door.

After a heavy sigh Matt stood. "Ran, here's where it begins. Everything changes for us once we set foot on that chopper."

They walked out of the conference room, and Peterson waved them out the side door of the police station, where Ruska waited to lead them to the helicopter.

Matt was right. Everything *was* about to change. She needed to face that reality. "I've never flown on one of these things. I'm not sure I want to. They don't have any wings."

"They've got wings." He chuckled. "But the wings move really fast. I've been in choppers a few times. It'll be too loud to talk, at least to talk privately."

"Keep your head down under the rotor," Ruska pointed upward as he led the way.

Looking at the dark-colored helicopter, hearing the whine as the blades began rotating, and pondering her future were more than she could handle. She had done as well as could be expected when they were attacked. But now she was about to step onto a menacing looking helicopter and sever ties, for an indefinite period of time, with everyone and everything she knew.

What about her parents? When they heard about her situation, would their attitude toward her change?

Randi was taking only one familiar thing into this new life, Matt Mathison. She had only known him for a few days, so how familiar was he? Her heart supplied the answer. Matt was her anchor. No matter what lay ahead of her, she needed his strength. She wouldn't trust him not to break her heart, but she knew he would die trying to protect her. He almost had. And, in his way, he cared for her. For now, that had to be enough.

Her immediate concern was the mechanical monstrosity sitting in front of her, acting like a fan somebody had tipped on its side. When she was a child, her parents told her not to stick her fingers into the protective mesh around the fan, but she was about to stick her whole body into this one.

Randi slowed, lagging behind Matt.

He reached back and tugged on her arm as they moved toward the steps at the helicopter's door.

With hair flying in her face, Randi reached for Matt's hand. She took it and pulled him close. "Matt, would you please hold—"

The noise grew louder.

He mouthed his words, "Can't hear you."

Now the whine of the engine and the whoosh of the rotor completely drowned their voices.

She glanced down at their clasped hands, then met his gaze. The expression on her face was probably pitiful looking to him. She hated showing her weakness.

Matt squeezed her hand and nodded. He helped her board, holding her hand the entire time.

The pilot pointed to the two rearmost seats, and they slid into them while Ruska took the seat ahead of them. A few seconds later, Peterson climbed on board and the engine revved.

When they took off, it seemed that every aspect of her ordeal that day, plus an ominous future, crashed down on her. Tears flowed until they spilled down her cheeks, and she didn't know how to shut them off. She laid her head on Matt's shoulder.

He brushed away the tears, curled an arm around her, and put his lips near her ear, whispering into it. His words came through clearly above the din of the climbing helicopter. "It'll be okay, Ran. I'll help you get through this."

Somehow, she believed him.

Randi fought her impulse to turn her head so their lips met. In the end, it wasn't the lack of privacy that stopped her, it was her fear that she would be irrevocably yielding her heart to a man she could not trust to protect it.

Time to buck up, Randi.

She wiped her tears and sat up in her seat, still gripping Matt's hand. Outside, well below them, a spectacular view of the snowcapped Olympic mountain's highest peaks moved slowly by, piercing her eyes with their white glare as they reflected the intense May sun framed by blue sky.

Before they cleared the mountains, the noise of the rotor, like an irritating percussion instrument, gave her a headache. A headache accompanied by nausea. This was *not* what she needed.

Randi Richards was a physically and mentally strong woman. But anyone who had observed her over the past two hours would think she was the female version of a wimp.

She had stared down world-class runners at the starting line of the fifteen hundred meters, when they gave her that who-do-you-think-you-are look, then she beat most of them. So why was today so different?

Danger and Matt, the unique ingredients of this day. The two were becoming inextricably intertwined in Randi's mind. She needed Matt because of the danger. When the danger was behind her, if that moment ever came, would she still need him?

The urge to vomit ended her musings.

Matt studied her face for a moment. "You're looking green, Ran." He pulled a bag from the pocket on the seat in front of them.

She took the bag, keeping the rest of her body still.

"You need to focus on something in the distance. Look out the window, eleven o'clock. See the Seattle skyline?"

The Space Needle loomed beyond the blue waters of Puget Sound. She focused on it and fought a fierce battle with nausea. Not until the helicopter landed at Boeing Field did she realize she had won.

After they touched down, the whining of the engine died and mercifully the pounding of the rotor ended. But her headache remained after the nausea faded.

Matt's eyes examined her face again. "You'll feel better soon. I puked right after my first chopper ride. Too much circling and that incessant pounding on my head."

Peterson twisted in his seat. "See the black sedan?" He pointed to a vehicle thirty yards away on the tarmac. "We're headed that way. You're about to meet some U.S. marshals, two of the best I know. I'm still working your case, but they will take over your protection. And if you need anything, ask them. They'll take care of it."

Matt grinned. "Service sounds pretty good here."

"Our service is better than a five-star resort."

Randi rubbed her temples. "So we can use a spa, and after that we get a massage?"

"Maybe our service is more like a four-star resort." He paused. "I'll be talking with you two, periodically. Mind the marshals. They know how to keep you safe." Peterson turned to Agent Ruska. "Hand them off to Wes and Cody." He strode away toward another car parked by one of the buildings lining the runway.

Agent Ruska led them at double-time pace to the car, nearly pushing them through the open door. He twirled a finger and the passenger-side window slid down. Ruska pushed his head inside. "Randi, Matt, your driver is Cody Randle. This runt here…" he pointed a thumb at the short, muscular man in the passenger seat, "…is Wesson Smith."

Matt grinned at the man. "So you gave us a real gunman to protect us, Smith and—"

Wesson cut in. "Call me Wes." He gave them a wide grin. "Too many people have too much fun with my name. It's good to meet you two."

"Yeah. We've heard a lot about both of you, but I have to say descriptions don't do you justice." Cody's eyes in the rearview mirror met hers.

"Cody fancies himself a ladies' man, but he's an officer and a gentleman."

"Unlike my partner, Wes," Cody added.

Wes motioned beyond the hill on their right. "We're headed to a motel in Redmond. It's too far out of the way for the bad guys to bother us. They generally stick to the I-5 corridor. And … we were instructed to stop at Freddy's en route."

"Thanks." Randi smiled despite their circumstances. The two marshals had a way of removing the tension. Maybe she *could* get through this with a little help. She intertwined her fingers with Matt's and leaned on his shoulder. Not because she needed to, but because she wanted to.

Chapter 16

Their big sedan turned off from a four-lane street on the edge of Redmond and pulled into a parking space at a decent-looking motel.

Randi watched with mixed emotions as Wes checked the surrounding area and then the two adjoining motel rooms before Cody let Matt and her out of the car. That the two marshals were thorough was comforting. That they needed to be was disconcerting.

With Wes prodding them, she hurried from the vehicle and stepped into the room, carrying her suitcase, a plastic bag from Fred Meyer. The bag held a change of clothing, some personal grooming items, and two pairs of underwear, which had been safely tucked into the bag before Wes stepped to the register to pay for her purchases.

The doorway to the adjacent room was open. That raised privacy questions, a whole host of them. Clearly the only privacy she would have would be in the bathroom.

This room had a king-sized bed. She stuck her head through the opened doorway and peered into the other room. There were two queen beds.

Three beds. Four people. How was that going to work?

Confined to a ten-by-thirty-foot room, she would soon be climbing the walls. Her near-term future looked more like prison than protection.

Randi wanted to throw open the door, find a road or a path, and run. Run until all of her concerns and fears were masked by fatigue and the endorphins that produce a runner's high.

Try as she might, she couldn't help wanting Matt to run with her. He was so close to being perfect for her that her heart ached with every thought of him. It ached for her, and it ached for Matt. For Matt because he would never be free from the Furies until he dealt with his baggage. For her, because she couldn't have the relationship she wanted with him until he dealt with his guilt, if he ever did.

Cody motioned Matt through the door to the adjoining room. Wes closed the outside door. "You'll have your own room. Either Cody or I will be awake at all times. If one of us needs a nap, we'll use the extra bed in Matt's room."

"Wes..." She drew a sharp breath when a claustrophobic feeling pressed in on her.

"What is it?"

"Do you have any idea how long we'll be stuck ... uh, how long we'll be here?"

"I wish I knew. Normally it's not long. A few days or so until folks at the office come up with a more permanent solution." He studied her for a moment.

She had grabbed her folded arms and squeezed, giving herself a bear hug. Randi took a breath and tried to relax.

"Randi, no one saw us bring you in here. It's paramount that there be no witnesses to your presence here, no opportunity for any loose lips. We can't take you or Matt out unless it's absolutely necessary."

She understood and nodded. But understanding didn't take away the claustrophobic feelings of being locked in a prison.

Wes cleared his throat. "It's normal when you're confined like this to feel a little cabin fever. Let us know if it gets to be a problem. We've seen it before. We can help."

"Thanks, Wes." She gave him a half-hearted smile and sat down on her king-size bed as Wes entered Matt's room.

"Knock. Knock. May I come in?" Matt stood in the doorway.

She waved him in. Any distraction would help right now, and Matt was certainly a distraction.

He sauntered into the room, stopping a short distance from her bed. "Ran, do you realize we're both still wearing our running clothes from this morning? You slipped on your t-shirt, but these shorts really logged some miles today."

"Yeah. I bought some other things, but I *like* my running suit, when it's not full of salt."

"And you love to run. When you ran, I could see it on your face, well ... the few times I managed to get ahead of you and look back I saw it."

"Yeah. I love it, Matt. I'm dying to go for a run right now."

"I knew the moment we met that you weren't an ordinary runner, somebody grinding out three to five miles a day just to keep in shape. You mentioned that you ran competitively."

She patted the bed beside her, and he sat down. "I ran track in high school. Texas A&M gave me a scholarship, and I ran on their women's team."

"They've got a strong track program. That's pretty impressive. What events did you run?"

"My best event was the 1500 meters."

"Were you any good?" He grinned at her.

She grabbed a pillow and smacked him over the head with it. "What do you think?"

"When I look at those legs, I think—"

"You can stop right there, Matt Mathison. This discussion isn't going to go that direction."

"Maybe not, but you can't control my thoughts?"

"Sounds like *you* can't control your thoughts either, and that's why we should change into something more ..." She stopped when a wave of concern rolled over Matt's face.

"I've really messed up your life. Wish I could change that. Ran, I'd do anything—"

She pressed her fingers over his lips, leaving them there a little longer than necessary to mute his words. "Changing the subject—"

"But I—"

"Matt, no. I meant what I said this morning. That subject is closed."

A sigh of resignation from Matt.

"I told you about my parents this morning. But you haven't said a word about yours. How ... how is your relationship with them?"

He stared down at the floor. "Maybe you should pick another subject."

"We're going to be together for who knows how long. Probably quite a while. Tell me, please? I'll only keep pestering you until ..."

Matt's words started barely above a whisper. "Mom and Dad knew that I got into drugs. They knew my life was going downhill fast. When it went too far down that hill, I broke off almost all contact with them. I called on Mother's Day, Father's Day, a few other times. Let them know I was alive, but that's all. I haven't seen them in two years." His voice crescendoed on the last two words.

She put a hand on his shoulder. "Then I'll pray that what's happening now changes all that. You know, something's going to show up in the newspapers about us, about the cartel. They'll be worried, Matt."

"Or just ashamed."

"Were they proud of you when you were leading the UW football team?"

"They told me they were."

"When they learn the truth about what you're doing now, they'll be proud of you again. You messed up, but you have the opportunity to change all of that."

"Not all of it. But it would feel good to be able to face them again and not to be an embarrassment to them."

How different Matt's problem with his parents was from hers. There was an end to his problem.

She lifted his chin and saw the eyes of an innocent boy, warm, caring, and a man who was handsome beyond belief.

She looked away from Matt across the room. It was dangerous for her to be so near Matt Mathison. He endangered her life and her heart. One of those she had no power to change. The other, she doubted that she could change and wasn't sure she wanted to.

What had they been talking about?

"And look at you." She scanned his face and upper body. "You're an incredible athlete, Matt. You should be—"

"No, Ran. I should not be playing football, if that's what you're thinking. The doctor said not to, but more importantly, I don't *deserve* to."

She reached across to his opposite shoulder and gave him a side hug. "You're wrong about the things you can do and what you deserve. So wrong."

"Knock, knock. Is everything alright in here?" Wes had stuck his head into the room. He looked at them and grinned. "It looks fine to me." His head disappeared.

She pulled her arm from Matt's shoulders. "See what you've done. People keep catching us doing ... things. They'll be talking about us like—"

"Maybe someday we can really give them something to talk about."

When they locked gazes, Randi, once again, felt the attraction between them. It pulled her toward Matt with a force that came from so deep inside her she couldn't understand it. And, right now, didn't have the means to resist it. She defined love as a voluntary commitment one person made to another to act lovingly. So what should she call this?

If it was chemistry, they certainly had it.

At the same time, other forces pulled Matt and her apart. But those forces she *could* understand. They came from the things Matt needed to remove from his life, like his paralyzing guilt.

"Got some news." Cody straddled the doorway. "Short night ahead of us. Word just came in that we found a home for you two, but we need to leave at 5:30 a.m. So, I suggest you get some rest."

"Okay." Matt pulled his feet to the edge of the bed to stand. "Goodnight, Randi."

She took his hand and squeezed. Maybe he would understand her feelings, even though she wasn't sure *she* understood them. "Pleasant dreams, Matt."

"Oh. They will be." A smile twisted the corners of his mouth as he turned to walk out of the room.

Her heart felt like a wishbone. Tonight, when they pulled on it, Matt ended up with the bigger half. But tomorrow ... she hadn't a clue.

Chapter 17

"All aboard. The car's leaving." The booming voice of Agent Peterson echoed through Randi's room. She glanced at the clock. 5:35 a.m.

With her plastic bag from Fred Meyer serving as her suitcase, Randi walked into Matt's room.

Matt grabbed a bag identical to hers. "Let's go check out our new digs."

After Randi and Matt slid into the rear seat, the big sedan pulled out of the motel, went a few blocks, then turned onto a small road.

"Are we headed for the mountains?" Randi looked out through the dark windows into the early dawn light and tried to get her bearings.

Peterson didn't reply.

If he thought that would end her questions, he had a lot to learn. "When are you going to tell us where we're going?"

"When we're about halfway there." Peterson glanced back at her.

She gave him an exaggerated frown. "So you don't trust us ... or even your driver?"

"Trust you, yes. Tell you, no. He or she who doesn't know information, can't leak it."

"Where are Wes and Cody?"

"You are full of questions this morning, young lady." Peterson sighed. "They'll be waiting for us when we arrive."

"Who watched us after they left?" she asked.

"Like I said, you are full of questions."

After fifteen minutes of negotiating a twisting, winding road through forestland, they drove into a valley, a patchwork of pastures dotted with dairy barns.

It was light now, and Randi saw a familiar-looking helicopter sitting in one of the pastures. The car turned onto a dirt road, then onto the grass, and stopped a few yards from the helicopter.

She stared at Peterson.

He stared back at her.

She cocked her head. "We're a little *over* halfway. Did you forget to tell us?"

"Patience. We're not yet halfway to our final destination."

Matt yawned. "I could have told you, Ran. Wherever we're going, it's not going to be that close to Seattle. Let's get on the whirlybird so I can finish my nap."

Her first ride in a helicopter hadn't gone well. Fear and nausea. Both maladies threatened to infect her again. "You can't go to sleep on me, Matt Mathison. I need you to ... you know."

"Whirlybirdophobia. She's got it, Peterson, but I benefit from it." Matt squeezed her hand.

"Just consider it a privilege you've earned."

Peterson slid to the door and opened it, giving them a crooked smile. "If for any reason you should want them to, Wes and Cody make very good chaperones."

"Come on. Randi and I are both adults."

Peterson stepped out of the car then stuck his head back inside. "I know, and that's why I'm letting you decide. Let's go, you two. Time to find a new nest for the lovebirds."

After Randi settled into her seat in the rear of the helicopter, with Matt's arm around her, the dread of their flight subsided.

The engine whined as it revved up. She leaned against Matt when they took off and closed her eyes.

A few moments later, light began seeping through her eyelids. Randi sat up and looked ahead to the east. The bright yellow glow tracing the outline of the Cascade peaks suddenly exploded into a golden ball. The climbing chopper had fast-forwarded the sunrise.

Her eyes closed and she sought the protection of Matt's shoulder again. Shielded from the sun, her world became only a warm fuzzy feeling that faded into peace.

Randi awoke to chatter from the front seat. She stretched a kink from her neck.

Matt was still asleep.

"Is that chopper following us or not?" It was Peterson's voice and he appeared to be talking to someone over the radio.

She listened. It sounded like Peterson was talking to Air Traffic Control. Was a passenger in an aircraft allowed to do that? Maybe FBI agents could.

Matt stirred and raised his head.

She spoke into his ear. "Someone may be following our flight."

Matt's eyes widened. "Peterson, what's up?"

He turned his head toward them. "Probably nothing, but another chopper seems to like our route as much as we do. We're trying to determine if—"

"He just turned south," the pilot said. "Headed for Yakima."

Peterson cleared with air traffic control. After terminating his radio call, he turned toward them again. "About where we're headed..."

She sat up in her seat. "Yes?"

"There's a big house on a hillside above Lake Chelan. It's owned by one of our ambassadors, and he's given the DOJ permission to use it for the next eighteen months. It's nearly 5,000 square feet, not including the three-car garage." Peterson studied them as if waiting for their reaction.

She tried to mask her surprise. Did Bill Gates have a summer home in Chelan? So much for cabin fever.

Peterson's brow wrinkled as he studied her face. "It has a spectacular view of the lake, Jacuzzi tubs in two of the bathrooms, and—"

"Does it have an indoor running track?" She grinned at Peterson and settled back in her seat.

His frown turned to a smile. "No. But, if I remember correctly, it has two treadmills."

Matt chuckled. "Can't have everything, Ran. But it sure beats two motel rooms."

Peterson's big smile faded. "You need to get used to this place, because it's going to be your home for an undefined period of time."

She sat up in her seat. "Do you mean undefined as in indefinitely?"

"No. I mean undefined as in I don't know when we'll catch certain cartel members and bring them to trial."

"Oh." The picture was jelling in her mind. They would have luxurious digs, but she wouldn't be running outside for a long time. Probably never at this place. She would go nuts.

"When we arrive, the marshals will go over some rules that you must follow if we're going to guarantee your safety." Peterson seemed to be studying them, gauging their reaction. "The rules may seem like overkill, but that's better than ... well, you get the idea."

"We'll be good, Peterson," Matt said. "I'll make sure Randi doesn't sneak out to run."

"I'm serious." His eyebrows rose. "You two aren't even going to be allowed in a room with opened curtains or—"

"Then why did you tell us about the view? This sounds like a really nice place, but will we get to see the sun at all?" SAD was well named. Hers was mild and easily cured by a little sun.

"I believe the exercise room doubles as a sun room. But about safety, the marshals will determine the shooting angles they need to worry about. Because the house sits on a bluff, I'm sure you'll have some spectacular views of the lake from safe locations in the house. You just won't get to stand near the big windows." Peterson glanced out the front window of the chopper, then back toward them. "Look to our left at about eleven o'clock and you'll see Lake Chelan. We're heading to the far side of it below the point jutting out into the lake. That's Wapato Point. You'll be able to see the house in a couple of minutes."

The lake appeared as a blue ribbon of water slicing through semi-arid land, then disappearing between snowcapped mountains to the north.

"Enjoy it as much as you can, because you'll be here until the trials are over. Try to think of it as your home and as a bit of compensation for the meanness of the cartel. If they weren't such a savage bunch, you might still be in that motel room."

Despite certain restrictions, she was impressed. Was God making a bad situation better for her?

She gave Matt a corner-of-the-eye glance. Maybe God had more in mind than she could imagine. But being with Matt, she could imagine a lot. And that's probably the only place she and Matt would ever really be together ... in her imagination. Unless Matt could give his guilt to God and get on with living.

Halfway across the lake, the helicopter started its descent. A red-brick house grew larger as the helicopter bore down on it. The house sat on a bench on the side of a high hill overlooking the lake. Five other houses sat on the bench too. Each looked like a multi-million-dollar home with a multi-million-dollar view.

A concrete pad lay south of the house, about fifty yards from the garage. The pad was centered on a lawn the size of a football field.

She tapped Peterson's shoulder. "Is that our landing pad?"

"That's it. Our own private airport."

They circled the house, and the pilot swung the chopper around in a one-eighty to land facing the lake.

Not knowing how long it might be before she got another look at the house from the outside, Randi tried to soak it all in, the manicured grounds and the magnificent setting.

There were two stories, but only a few gabled windows on the upper floor. The house was long with a forty-five-degree bend in the middle and a three-car garage at the end nearest the landing pad.

Matt spoke softly into her ear. "We'll be living like the rich and famous."

She was neither rich nor famous, but Matt? That might have been his house if he hadn't gotten hurt. "At least we can enjoy playing rich for a while."

By the time the rotor slowed and the door opened, Cody, Wes, and two other men had positioned themselves by the helicopter.

Peterson motioned for her and Matt to get out. "We'll do introductions inside."

A long hedge separated the landing area and its lawn from the house and driveway. The four marshals surrounded her and Matt, herding them at a brisk pace across the grass, through a gap in the hedge, and toward an open door.

The lake disappeared from view when they crossed the paved, circle driveway and approached the door. The setting and the house were beautiful. This was a dream home that dwarfed anything she ever expected to live in.

The sunshine poured in through the open door. She stepped through it then stopped, basking in the warm sunlight.

"Hair's on fire." Matt's mouth twisted into a big smirk.

"Move ahead, away from the door." Peterson's voice.

She stepped ahead. That ought to douse the fire.

Matt moved beside her.

The latch clicked behind them, then the clunk of a large deadbolt. Peterson had closed and locked the door, cutting off the sun and closing the door on a chapter of her life. But it opened a new chapter, a chapter full of luxury and confinement.

Peterson stepped around her and Matt and gestured to the four men who stood facing them. "Randi, Matt, meet Marshals Jake Andrews and Andy Taylor."

After they exchanged handshakes, Cody stepped out of the entryway toward an adjacent room. He turned and motioned for them to follow. "I'm going to give you two the rules of the house. You need to pay attention because following these will keep you safe. If you choose to break them, we can't guarantee you'll be alive to testify at any trials."

Matt whispered in her ear. "Sounds like Cody. All business and not above a little intimidation."

She turned her head toward Matt. "A *little* intimidation? He's trying—"

"Are you listening, Ms. Richards?" Cody's scowl ended her conversation with Matt.

"Yeah. Sorry." She scanned the room they had entered. Her whole apartment would fit inside with room left over.

Cody stared at her for a moment from the center of the room, then continued. "With time you'll experience the tendency to grow lax. Don't. The danger to you grows exponentially with time as the cartel continues its search for you. Do you see the yellow tape at the far side of the great room?"

Waist-high cones strung with florescent yellow tape formed an arc around the series of large windows lining the lake side of the big room. The bold black lettering on the tape repeated the message. POLICE LINE DO NOT CROSS.

She nodded to Cody.

"Wherever you see yellow tape, you are not to go into the cordoned off area. We've determined these areas are unsafe. Also, never enter a room that has drapes or blinds opened, except the great room, which we've carefully marked with tape."

Randi walked up to the tape.

Cody tracked her. "That's close enough."

"But I can't see the shore of the lake from here."

"That's by design. The shore is less than a thousand yards from here. Well within a sniper's range."

He must be exaggerating the danger to frighten her. "So how far can a sniper shoot accurately?"

"Ms. Richards..." Cody stared into her eyes with an intensity that caused her to step back near Matt. "... at one thousand yards, a sniper can shoot you between the eyes ... every time. A really good sniper, with the proper equipment, can kill you from twenty-five hundred yards." He turned and pointed at the dark blue, glassy waters of Lake Chelan. "He can kill you from a boat in the middle of the lake."

Chapter 18

Randi opened her eyes and tried to get her bearings. Her body lay diagonally across a king-size bed. It was *her* king-size bed in her king-size bedroom. The place she would likely be sleeping for the next several months.

With the curtains closed, the room was dark, lit only by the yellow light leaking in around the edges of the heavy curtains.

Yellow light meant the sun was up. She could use some sunshine, but that meant going to the sunroom and opening the skylight to its clear-glass setting.

She opened her bedroom door and checked the hallway. No one there. But two cardboard boxes sat in the hall beside her doorway. She lifted a lid on the topmost box. Clothing, pictures— someone had brought the things she requested from her apartment.

Peterson had done what he promised. But her things hadn't come by helicopter. She would have heard.

The boxes slid easily into her room. After closing her door, she rummaged through the folded clothes, wondering what she should wear. She wanted to check the weather first. Not that it mattered much with a perpetual seventy-two-degree climate controlled by the furnace, air conditioning and, from the feel of the air, a humidifier.

Her bathrobe lay in the bottom of the first box. She slipped into it and wandered down the hall, turning in at the great room. Randi stepped near the tape and looked out the windows.

The morning sun beamed over the roof of the house, lighting the lake to the west and turning the calm water into a long, wide mirror that reflected the Cascade peaks with their small snowcaps that hadn't yet melted in the summer-like conditions.

It was only May third, but summer had arrived in Chelan Washington, thanks to the El Nino and the accompanying drought.

What about the drought in her life? Right now, no job in Meteorology. Possibly no career in her field either, depending on the outcome of the search for cartel members and the cartel's degree of vindictiveness.

So what did her future hold now? Uncertainties for sure. And what about Matt? If only he would stop rolling in the muck of unworthiness and start acting like the man God meant him to be, the man she believed he could be again.

If he didn't come around soon, she would approach that subject, regardless of its sensitivity.

After a few moments gazing out the windows until the urge to slip into her running gear and charge out the door became a strong temptation, she wandered into the kitchen. Randi opened the refrigerator and pulled out a half-gallon carton of milk. A large pantry occupied most of the adjacent wall. She opened its big doors and spotted a box of granola. When she turned toward the counter on the opposite side of the room, her eyes stopped on an eighteen-inch-high, metallic device.

In the center of the counter, sat a De'Longhi, the Cadillac of latte machines.

The instructions were taped on the side the machine, so why not? She found a bag of coffee beans in the pantry and followed the directions.

While the machine ground, whirred and made bubbling noises, another sound came from behind her.

She whirled toward it.

Matt stood in the kitchen doorway watching her. Dressed in cargo shorts and a polo shirt, he looked nice.

No. He looked like he did after he tackled her, magnificent. "I didn't hear you come in. Would you like a latte?"

"Sure. What kind?" Matt approached, eyes on her, not the machine.

"I'm not sure. Everything is automatic on this machine. Hopefully, whoever programmed it has our taste." She slid a cup into place.

In a few moments, it filled.

"But I think we have to put in our own flavoring." She positioned a second cup. "Matt, did you find a box outside your room this morning?"

"Yes. It had the rest of the things I asked them to bring from my rental house."

"Did it have your manuscript in it?"

"Yes."

"So do you plan to write while we're here?"

"If I get in the mood."

She sat down at the table across from him and slid a cup his way. "You write romantic suspense. Can't you get in the mood here? There certainly is enough suspense—yellow tape, snipers ..."

Matt's gaze had followed her continuously since she spotted him in the kitchen.

Randi studied his face and nearly gasped when she recognized the look in his eyes. His longing look.

He was getting too close for comfort. Far too close until Matt finished what he had started a few months ago, opening his unfettered heart to God's forgiveness. Then, perhaps, opening his heart to her?

"I could do without the suspense. But until the DOJ suspends it, I ..."

He didn't finish. He didn't need to.

She could see it in his eyes. Matt wanted the romance, but he wasn't going to let it happen. "You're not being punished, Matt, only protected. You act like your life is over, or on hold."

"It *is* on hold, indefinitely."

"Constrained a bit, but not on hold. You still have the freedom to make a lot of decisions about your life. Your situation isn't any different from mine."

"Ran, it *is* different."

"No, Matt. Think about it. My life is being planned for me. My career ... that's out of my control. Yeah, I'm struggling with that. And I could use your help with—"

"I wouldn't be any help. Only a hindrance. And my future has a great big question mark tattooed on it. It *will* have until the federal prosecutor decides what to do with me. Then I have to wait and see how the cartel reacts to—"

"No, you don't. All you need to do is accept the complete forgiveness you've been given. Instead, you just wallow in your guilt and misery until you're not..." She grabbed her coffee cup, strode from the kitchen, and headed down the hallway for her room. Her anger only partially masked the ache in her heart.

"Randi ..."

She couldn't let herself turn around. Randi hurried down the hallway, wishing she could distance herself from Matt. Not have to ride the rollercoaster of emotions he seemed to put her on.

She needed his help. She'd admitted as much. A few days ago, he said he could never reject her, but he wasn't willing to be there for her. At that time, she had trusted him with her life. But with the marshals protecting them, she didn't need to rely on Matt for her safety. Maybe she needed to stop relying on Matt for anything, because Matt wasn't reliable.

Until Matt was spiritually and emotionally well, he would only continue hurting her. For the rest of their time in this mansion, she must keep her distance from him. She would be polite, but distant ... as distant as 5,000 square feet allowed.

Chapter 19

May 31, four weeks later

In a coffee shop in Wenatchee, Zambada sat, staring across the street at the old motel ... waiting. Where was Bennie? Probably feeding his face or playing video games.

But the truth was Zambada couldn't blame Bennie for their being stuck in this—what did the gringos in those fettuccine westerns call it? A one-horse town?

If the *great Zambo* had killed Matt Mathison, they would all be back in Tijuana living the good life. But Matt, hamstrung with that girl, had eluded him. Matt would pay for breaking his word to the organization and then for the damage to Zambada's reputation.

Now, his boss, Arellano, was angry. He had told Zambada, in graphic detail, how his head would roll if he didn't stop Matt and his auburn-haired Barbie from testifying against any member of the organization. Law enforcement in Hicksville, Washington had managed to catch three of their men, and rumor had it that a grand-jury had been convened—all because of Matt and Barbie.

"Barbie." He laughed. The girl was tough, and she ran like a gazelle. Maybe Matt escaped *because* of the girl, not in spite of her. Regardless, Matt appeared to be taken with her.

Now that Zambada had bee-lined the safe house by following the chopper several times on different segments of its flights, he knew the house's location. Once he traced them to Chelan, the helicopter pad beside the house was a dead giveaway. And, if Benjamin would get his fat rear end over here and let him into the room, they could finalize his scheme for dispensing with Matt Mathison and the girl.

Matt had a weakness. He had shown it when he protected the girl while Zambada shot at them. Perhaps he need only take one person, Barbie, and he could get them both.

A car turned into the motel driveway and parked in front of their room. Bennie.

Zambada stood and dropped a five spot on the table. He headed out the door, crossed the street, and rapped on Bennie's window. "It's about time you got here. The big fish is running. Time is spinning off the reel. When we are out of it, *pop* goes the line and the big marlin, Matt, swims free."

Bennie grinned and pointed a pudgy index finger at Zambada's face. "Ricardo, you worry too much."

"You can stop the Ricardo Montalban stuff. I've heard enough of it."

Bennie slid out of the car and shut the door. "But, Zambo, everyone say you look and talk like him, ees true ... even Arellano."

"Bennie, you sound like Ricky Ricardo."

"I take that as a compliment." Bennie unlocked the room door.

When he stepped in, the room wreaked of cleaners and disinfectants. It was not as unpleasant as the pine-scented cleaners used in the prison, a place he would avoid at any cost. Still, after a few minutes his eyes watered. After a few more, he felt like someone had sandpapered his sinuses.

The manager was obviously doing his best with the old motel, but Zambada normally stayed in finer establishments. However, his current assignment required him to remain inconspicuous in Wenatchee tonight and to have easy access to the highway running northward to Chelan.

Bennie, Arellano's most talented and trusted geek, had chosen this place before Zambada arrived, and the rotund hacker now sat at a desk alternately typing and clicking using a top-of-the-line laptop.

Zambada peered over Bennie's shoulder at several windows tiled on the screen. "Bennie, tell me again why you picked this dump."

"They still use hardwired Internet connections, Zambo. Nearly everyone is gone to wireless."

His gut knotted. Geeks and their technology irritated and frustrated him. Bennie's big rear end hanging off the chair begged to be kicked. Bennie wasn't vindictive, but still Zambada's life was going to depend on this man. "You haven't answered my question."

"Okay. For my computer-challenged amigo, I explain. People who run hotels know nothing about wireless routers. If router has problem, guests lose Internet access. If router goes flakey, we lose our connection, and our video feed—"

"Okay. Okay. You have made your point. Enough geek speak. Maybe I can stand this room for one night ... *if* there are no bedbugs."

Bennie twisted his head around, giving him a toothy grin. "There are no bedbugs in my bed. But you, Zambo, must take your chances with zee other bed." Bennie scratched the seat of his pants, and chuckled.

"We have other worries. Our window of opportunity is rapidly closing. What did you find out about the video surveillance system at the safe house?"

"Luis read the manufacturer's label from side of one of cameras using his high-powered binoculars. I have their router dancing to rhythm of a song I wrote."

"Are you certain you can get the video feed tonight?"

"I get it tonight, and then tomorrow night, ees rerun season."

"Are you sure you can be ready by tomorrow night?"

Bennie grinned at him again. "It pays to buy only best hacking tools from experts, zee Russians. I don't trust Chinese, or Eastern European hackers, or hackers anywhere in Middle East." He gestured with a raised index finger. "You watch. I gain access to host computer for surveillance system in a few minutes. I already talk with a tech support person from system manufacturer, so I know how their software works. Intercepting video stream and grabbing video files ... ees child's play." Bennie swiveled his chair to face him. "But, Zambo, the router here ees old LinkSys. Solid as rock, but no racehorse. I can only guarantee one video stream. If I try to send feed for two cameras, they will see intermittent video failure."

"Only one camera." Zambada pinched his chin. "Can I move about the house?"

"No. I already see their cameras and their video. Hallways are monitored."

Zambada folded his arms. "This complicates things, but I will not risk getting caught or killed by letting them see me."

This break-in had too many constraints. But he'd dealt with them before. "If the hallways are out, I can only enter one room, through one window. This is not good."

Bennie shook his head. "No, not good. But we have plan B."

Zambada nodded. "We go to plan B. Capture the girl. Call Luis and let the others know."

He drew Bennie's attention. "You called this child's play. They have nine cameras outside the house. Who knows how many inside? How can you say this is child's play?"

Bennie reached out and patted Zambada's arm.

He jerked both arms away from the short, fat man's reach. No one touched Zambada without an invitation.

Bennie gave him a condescending smirk.

The heat of Zambada's temper stopped a few degrees short of rage. Bennie was lucky this time.

"How this ees child's play? Let me see. Does Zambo want nerd's description or simpleton's?"

"Someday, Bennie, you push me too far and I—"

"We should not conjecture about future, except future of safe house and two people who are in it, zee traitor and zee beautiful senorita. I give you short version, Zambo.

Video stream of each camera ees controlled separately by management software. I simply pick stream I want and grab ees video file. My software edits file. At appropriate time, we stream altered file to management software and *voila*, zee U.S. Marshal watches a rerun of his favorite show."

"But the exact time ... we don't know that yet."

"Not to worry. I use local time supplied in real-time from host computer. They won't know ees rerun, trust me."

"I *am* trusting you. My life depends upon your hack, Bennie. Tell me what might possibly go wrong."

"Zee weather tonight could be different than weather tomorrow night. But in Chelan on a summer night, only wind varies. It will not be a problem. The other complication is controllable camera. But cameras we are considering are all non-PTZ."

"Enough nerdish. Translate."

"They cannot pan, tilt, or zoom. Camera just points where it points, always showing same area." Bennie stroked his chin a few times. "Oh, there ees possibility that one of marshals might walk in front of camera. They expect to see him, but they don't."

"Then I would kill him, take the marshal's place, and let them have a glimpse of me."

"Reesky. I do not envy you, Zambo. You have much to do to get in and out again with a hostage. I think I prefer my role. Hide and hack."

"We know the house layout from the contact Luis made with the builder. But the actual bedrooms where Matt Mathison and the girl sleep—that is a gamble, but one I will win." He pounded his palm with his fist. "I must get one of them in the room that I enter, hopefully the girl. When I leave, Bennie, you must turn off the sensor—" Zambada smashed his fist on the desk and spewed the dregs of his vocabulary into the room. "Stupid! Stupid! That will not work."

Bennie leaned away from Zambada and his angry outburst. "What do you mean, Zambo?"

"Here's how we will do it." Zambada brought his folded hands to his face and tapped his chin while he concentrated. "Luis said the marshals go up and down the stairway, but not Matt and his Barbie." He pulled folded papers from his pocket, opened them, and spread them out on the desk. "If you were Barbie, which bedroom would you want?"

Bennie scanned the plans and pointed to the bedroom nearest the garage. "This one has private bath with Jacuzzi. I think you find Barbie there."

"I agree. That is the room I will enter. You must control the video to the camera covering that window and disable any sensors on that bedroom window. Can you do that with this system?"

"Once I complete hacking system, I can make it play La Cucaracha if you want me to."

"This is very important, Benjamin. I need you to tell me how you know which sensor goes to which part of the house."

"You break my heart, Zambo. You do not trust Bennie? Okay. I read sensor location from database zee application software uses to store locations of all sensors."

"And you will tell me if you have any problem?"

"Of course, Zambo. Your work ees my bread and butter. I would not put you in danger by intention or stupidity."

"Then do one more thing for me. After you hack the video system, monitor the perimeter and see if there is any pattern to their visual checks. Like when the marshal walks the perimeter of the house. I want to ensure no marshal comes out as I am going in."

"Consider it done. But how is it you get away with zee girl? That I do not understand. I think maybe you should pay me in advance." Bennie smirked again.

"Maybe instead of you hacking the system, I hack you ... with my machete." He raised his voice hoping the intimidation would stop the annoying banter.

"I only mean to be funny." Bennie spun his chair around and faced the laptop. "I need quiet time to finish hacking computer and management software. Would you please—"

"I am going to bed now." Zambada turned toward his bed and cringed when he thought about bedbugs. "Hack all night. That's what you usually do, isn't it?"

"It depends. But, Zambo, a certain thing would ensure my success tonight."

"Tell me what you want."

"Go to the convenience store across the street and bring Bennie three bags of those flaming hot lime snacks? Like these." He held up an empty bag.

Zambada blew out a blast of air. "I will do this once. But someday soon you will have a heart attack and die. Probably just when I need your services." He paused. "Bennie ... perhaps I should replace you with Luis."

Bennie emitted a belly-shaking laugh. "The only hack Luis knows is hacky sack."

Zambada glared at Bennie.

It drew another annoying laugh. "I take my cholesterol medication faithfully. Bennie will be around for many more years. But average lifespan of an assassin ... not so long. I will outlive you, Zambo."

Chapter 20

June 1

For the past four weeks Randi had been careful to avoid being alone with Matt.

At first, Matt made overtures several times a day.

After a week of consistent rebuffs, Matt withdrew. They only saw each other at meal times.

Wes tried to play counselor, to get the two of them back into a better relationship. But he didn't understand the deep issue that divided Matt and her.

But avoiding Matt was becoming more difficult, uncomfortable, and unnatural. She feared her heart was to blame more than her head. The isolation in the big house wore on her. Last night she'd tossed and turned most of the night, catching only a few hours of sleep early in the morning.

Tired but unable to sleep, she sat up in bed and looked at the window beside her. The light around her curtains indicated the sun was up. She might as well be up too. Maybe Matt had already eaten breakfast. If not, she could get a cup of coffee and return to her room until Matt vacated the kitchen.

She dressed, brushed her teeth, ran the brush through her hair enough to be presentable, then headed down the hallway to the kitchen.

Matt stood in front of the latte machine finishing up a steaming drink that smelled wonderful. When he turned toward her, he held two cups. He sat one on one side of the breakfast table and took a seat on the other side with his drink in hand.

His eyes looked tired as they traced a path from her to the cup on the opposite side of the table. "Please. Sit down for a minute."

It wasn't a good idea, but that sad, puppy dog look in his eyes was hard to refuse. She sat, picked up the steaming cup of coffee and took a sip, avoiding any further looks into those pitiful looking eyes.

Matt reached across the table and laid his hand over hers.

She drew a sharp breath but couldn't move her hand. No. She didn't *want* to move her hand.

"Randi," his voice was low and soft, "I made the biggest mistake of my life."

She began steeling her emotions for what was coming. "Dealing drugs was a big mistake. You knew there would be consequences."

"I wasn't talking about dealing drugs. That was a mistake. But it was small compared to ... to hurting you."

"Forget it. I'm over it." She had just point-blank lied to Matt. A knot formed in her gut. "We have to get along here for who knows how long. I'm not going to get on another emotional roller coaster with you, Matt. I couldn't stand that."

"But we do need to get along. If they think it's not working with us both here, they'll separate us."

The knot in her stomach tightened. She met his gaze. "How do you know that?"

"I heard Peterson telling Wes to let him know if there were, you know, problems between us. You know how Wes has been trying to play counselor." Matt's eyes pleaded even more than his words.

She looked away.

"Please, look at me, Ran. Don't you see where this is leading? Someday, near the end of the trials, we'll be offered the Witness Protection Program. They have to do it. Cartels are unrelenting, unforgiving—"

"Unforgiving? Like you think God is with you?" She gave her head an exaggerated shake, flinging her hair from side to side. "You need to get from hearing the rooster crow to hearing 'feed my sheep'." This wasn't going to end well. It was time for her to leave. "You need to deal with your stuff, Matt. Not for my sake, but for yours." Randi stood and strode out of the room, trying to shove Matt's concerned look from her mind.

She entered the great room, headed for the adjoining hallway leading back to her room, barely aware of Cody and Wes on her left staring out a window on the mountain side of the house. Was something out of the ordinary happening?

"Randi ..." Matt's voice came from behind her.

Matt was chasing her. *That* was out of the ordinary.

She couldn't stop. Couldn't talk to him now. But something deep inside told her she must stop.

Wes spun around toward her. "Randi, get back! We think someone's on the hill above us."

She tried to process his words.

Wes and Cody had the blinds open. They weren't supposed to—

"Randi!" A strong arm took her down to the floor.

She landed on a thick area rug.

Matt's body covered her head and upper torso, pinning her to the floor.

"Blinds are closed!" Cody yelled. "Wes, watch these two, I'm going up the hill." Cody ran to the back door.

"Matt, would you please let me up?" She pushed on Matt's arm. It didn't move.

"Not yet. Not until they say it's safe." His strong arms constricted.

She couldn't move. A sharp pain pierced her ankle. "My ankle. You—"

"Cody just gave the all clear signal." Wes turned from the door to face them. "You can let her up, but both of you head back into the kitchen and stay there until we know for sure what's going on outside." Wes motioned toward the kitchen door. "Do it now, Matt!"

Randi gasped when Matt scooped her up in his arms. He ran to the doorway, then turned sideways to carry her through it into the kitchen.

"My ankle's fine now. I just tweaked it. Put me down."

When he reached the middle of the room, he stopped and met her hostile gaze.

The concern in Matt's intense eyes, a look bordering on horror, stabbed her heart. He had shielded her body with his own, doing everything in his power to protect her.

She couldn't be mad, couldn't even pretend to be. "Oh, Matt. What am I going to do about you?" Her heart and her head had two different answers to that question.

She intended to lay her head on his shoulder, but Matt's powerful arms lifted her up until their faces were only inches apart.

He stopped moving.

She didn't.

Randi raised her head and pressed her lips against Matt's. She slipped her arms around his neck and kissed him. It was long. It was sweet. And it wasn't just a kiss of appreciation. But the kiss was mostly hers.

Then suddenly, the kiss changed. This was a different Matt. A man who could lead a group of warriors down the field and across the goal line. After he pulled his lips from hers, Randi put her head on his shoulder and whispered. "Matt ... maybe you should put me down now."

"Sorry, Ran. I forgot about—" He lowered his arms, let her slide down onto her feet, and took her hand. "What's happening out there, Wes?"

Wes stepped to the kitchen doorway with his cell phone on his ear. He stopped and snapped it closed. "It was some South American tourist with a camera, shooting pictures, not bullets. Didn't speak much English"

Matt's face grew taut. "Did he speak Spanish or Portuguese?"

"Spanish. But he's harmless." Wes's hand waived the issue away. "Had his wife and a kid with him in the car."

Matt relaxed a bit, sighed, and mumbled something Randi couldn't distinguish.

Was Matt still concerned? The incident was disquieting, but the changes it had brought for Matt and her made the uneasiness a small thing.

Wes shook his head, frowning at them. "Cody and I need to be more careful about the windows. If we need to use them for surveillance, we'll put our yellow tape across the doorway. If you see yellow tape, you two are not to enter the room until we remove it."

Matt dipped his head. "We understand."

Randi pulled Matt further back into the kitchen, out of sight of Wes, trying to make sense of the flurry of events, trying to come up with an appropriate response. "Matt, you threw me on the floor, practically sat on top of me, picked me up and ..."

"I guess I did. Everything you said and ... a little more."

"Well ... what do you have to say for yourself?"

"You ... uh ... you're heavier than you look, Ran."

"What? Are you saying—"

"Muscle weighs a lot more than fat, and there's not a bit of fat on you."

"So I'm a big, heavy, burly—"

"No. You're perfect. But I couldn't stand the thought of a bullet doing anything to change that. And then ..."

"Yeah ... and then ..." Her voice was nearly gone, hardly more than a whisper, overrun by the thought that had entered her mind as if someone else had placed it there at precisely this moment. The thought was revealing, convicting, and it defined the events of the past few weeks with a clarity that had eluded Randi until now.

I was wrong. Terribly wrong.

She had been selfishly waiting for Matt to become the perfect man for her. But God had brought them together so she could help Matt be the man he was meant to be, the man God had in mind when He created Matt. And she believed Matt could help her wounded heart to heal, enabling her to forgive and love her parents.

Matt needed her and she needed him.

As Randi had speculated, running into each other was no mere coincidence. It was the kind of coincidence only a good and loving God could create.

His hands cupped her cheeks. "Ran, you faded away."

"I'm back now." She looked into his face, seeing it in a new perspective. His face drew her warmest smile.

He raised his eyebrows. "Who's back? The woman who kissed me or the one who stomped out of the room a few moments ago? I need to know before I turn you loose and you whack—"

"It's the one who kissed you. The other woman's dead and buried."

"Good. Let's hold a wake and celebrate."

Chapter 21

Matt stood facing Randi, their kitchen kiss still fresh on his mind. He looked down at their hands, palms-to-palms, fingers interlaced, like their lives and their future. It was what he wanted and what he needed.

He looked up when Wes returned to the kitchen.

"Matt, you know the three Tijuana cartel members the FBI caught on the Peninsula?"

Matt nodded.

"They just caught another one. Peterson needs you to tell him if they've got the assassin, Zambada."

Matt peered deeply into Randi's eyes and squeezed her hand. "With romantic thrillers there's always something happening."

Randi blushed and stepped behind him. Probably blocking her face from Wes's view.

He turned toward Wes and released Randi's hand. "So where do we go to identify them?"

"Upstairs. We have secure collaboration software. They rolled it out to all the field offices last year. It's running on my laptop upstairs in the office. Anything you can put on a computer screen we can show remotely."

Matt turned to Randi. "We need your eyes too. I doubt that they got Zambada, and we only caught glimpses of the goons in the blue sedan. But you saw as much as me."

"I'm coming, Matt. Those guys nearly killed us. I want a shot at them too."

Matt took her hand and pulled her along behind him as they walked up the stairs, his heart beating like this was eight or nine flights of stairs. He took a deep breath and slowly exhaled. Maybe he wasn't over the kiss yet, either. "Let's go see if they've got Zambada or nada."

He escorted her into the office.

The room was furnished like an executive's office. Being in the house of an ambassador, that's what it probably was.

Cody and Jake had focused on the screen of an expensive looking laptop, but Cody had a cell phone planted in his ear. "They're here, Pete. I'm switching to my speakerphone." He plugged his phone into a small docking device.

"This is Peterson. Can everyone hear me?"

"Loud and clear." Cody motioned for Matt to sit in the chair centered on the laptop's screen.

"First," Peterson said, "here's a high-resolution picture of suspect number one. Do you recognize him, Matt?"

A swarthy man with a scar on his nose and close-cropped hair. Not Zambada.

"Ran does that look like one of the men in the sedan?"

She leaned in closer to the screen. "Yeah. He's the driver. I got a good look at him."

Matt leaned toward the cell phone. "Did you hear that, Peterson?"

"We heard. But tell us about this next one."

A dark-complexioned man with a short mustache appeared, once again in high resolution.

"He's ugly and scary looking. But I'm not sure," Randi said.

"But I am, Peterson. He was with Zambada at the meeting where they made the offer to me. I saw him again the day Zambada ran me through his training course. Just before I bailed out."

Randi leaned over his shoulder and studied the man's face again. "Yeah. Now I remember him. He was in the sedan when we passed it on our way to the weather station."

"Hmmm. One of the gunmen? Could you testify to that in a court of law?"

Randi sucked in a deep breath and squeezed Matt's shoulder. "Yeah, I can do that."

"And I can definitely connect him to the Tijuana Cartel," Matt added.

"Good. Two down and—"

Matt cut in. "And Zambada still to go."

"Thank you, guys. That's all for today."

Wes pulled his phone out of the docking station, looked at Matt and Randi, and pointed at the door. "You can go back to the kitchen." He grinned at them. "Or whatever."

Randi pulled Matt from the room and strode toward the stairway. "Wes saw us, Matt."

"So. I'm not ashamed of what I did."

"I'm not either. But something that intimate you just ... you can't—"

"It was a kiss, Ran."

"But I've never felt like that before."

This was getting interesting. "Felt like what?"

"Like we might actually need Wes and Cody to be our chaperones."

Chapter 22

"It's beginning isn't it, Matt?" Randi reached the bottom of the stairway and waited for him. "The arrests, the trials, our testimony, then the great unknown. But..."

He looked at her, waiting.

She sought the words to describe her strange blend of emotions. "Have you ever tried to make one of those healthy smoothies?"

"Yeah." He chuckled. "I learned right away to put enough berries in to cover-up the wheatgrass. But nothing covers up the kale."

"That's what my life feels like—a smoothie. I don't know if it is a healthy one or not. But when all of the ingredients are blended together, including the bad stuff, something wonderfully delicious masks everything else, even the wheatgrass and kale." She looked into his eyes and smiled. "Sometimes I'm surprised by the flavor that dominates."

"So I'm just a flavor in your smoothie? You can enjoy me until the straw makes that gurgling sound, then I'm all gone?"

"No, Matt. But there is a lot of wheatgrass in my life, and you make the whole thing taste like strawberries."

"Ran, you know what they say about strawberries?"

"I don't think I want to hear it." Her face grew hot. Her ears too. She looked away.

"If you want to be healthy ..." He motioned toward the exercise room. "Wanna have a treadmill race?"

"Neither of them goes past ten miles per hour. I'll be so out of shape when we leave this place that I won't be able to make it up those two hundred steps to the beach."

He quickly scanned her from head to foot. "I doubt that. But if you don't want to run, we could go back into the kitchen and—"

"No. That's reserved for special times. We're *not* going to do that several times a day. I told you why, Mr. Mathison."

"Well, have *you* got any ideas?"

"We could critique your manuscript."

He shook his head. "It's not ready for that yet. Needs more layering. It would just put you to sleep."

"Romantic thrillers are hardly the stuff that puts a person to sleep. My writing on the other hand..."

"I've got an idea for this evening." He took her hand. "Let's explore the house together. We've been here for several weeks and still have seen less than half the rooms. Maybe we can find a wardrobe and escape to another world."

"That wasn't such a good place to go. Permanent winter. Okay. Exploring it is. But right now, I'm going running. At ten miles-per-hour, it'll take two hours to get in a good workout."

It wasn't a strong runner's high, but ninety minutes at ten miles-per-hour felt good. The Jacuzzi afterward felt even better. It had nearly put her to sleep. She slipped into her robe and stretched out on the bed for a moment, more relaxed than she had been since they arrived at the safe house.

Randi tried to open her eyes. They weren't cooperating. When they finally popped open, it took a few minutes to get her bearings. She looked at the clock on the stand beside her bed. 5:00 p.m. She had slept for four hours.

Would Matt think she was avoiding him again? No. Not after the fireworks this morning.

She took her time getting ready, selected one of her sundresses, and then went looking for Matt.

"You really zonked out." Wes grinned at her when she stepped into the hallway. "I was just checking to see if you wanted takeout for dinner tonight. Cody found this fantastic little teriyaki spot in town. It makes sauce that can cauterize your nose just by smelling it."

"Cauterize my nose? I think I just lost my appetite."

"Matt sent me to check on you." Wes's voice raised a semi-tone or two? "Said your room was off limits to him. Did you two have another—"

"No. Everything is fine. He's just being, uh … prudent."

"Prudent is good. Changing the subject, have you changed your mind about the teriyaki?"

"Sure. I'm game. How hot is this stuff, really?"

"It comes from one to five stars. Three is a slow burn. Four is marginally edible. Don't even think about—"

"Get me a four. And where did you say Matt was?"

"I didn't. But he's in the great room. Exploring, I think."

She hurried down the hallway and stopped in the arched doorway leading into the room.

A huge wall unit covered one wall of the great room. The rich, dark-oak structure housed a large, flat-screen TV, stereo components, books, and drawers.

Matt had opened a drawer and busily thumbed through its contents.

"You didn't wait for me. What are you doing, spying on the ambassador?"

He continued to thumb through the drawer. "You wouldn't believe the stereo system. Or the music collection this guy has." He closed the drawer and turned to face her. "Wow." He took a second, longer look. "What's the occasion?"

She realized the green cotton dress contrasted nicely with her hair color. But Matt's reaction—was the sundress too bare or were the looks she was getting the new normal for him? "We were going exploring *after* dinner, but it appears you jumped the gun."

"Only for this room. But since you're all dressed up for—"

"Matt, I'm not dressed up."

He scanned her for the third time. "Except for the hair color, when I turned around I could've sworn I was looking at a real, live—"

"You'd better not say Barbie." She stepped into the warm sunshine streaming in through the big windows.

"Barbie? Not with red hair that could set me on fire if I tried to—"

"Matt..." she grabbed a pillow from the sofa and chased him around the room. After he avoided several swings of the pillow, Matt whirled and wrapped her up in his arms, pinning the arm holding the pillow.

She stood in Matt's arms, face to face with him, breathing hard from the chase.

"Ran, you are so beautiful." His eyes spoke the same message.

"I'm glad you think so, but please don't call me Barbie. Some of the guys on the track team tormented me with that until I graduated. Those were some Aggies I really wanted to gig."

"Huh?" He stepped back, putting his hands on her shoulders. "Oh, I get it. Gig'em Aggies. Beautiful and clever."

He motioned toward the wall unit. "The stereo system is an audiophile's dream. And look at the floor. That's got to be a thirty-foot square of polished hardwood in the center of the room. Does it give you any ideas?"

She looked at the floor, then eyed Matt from the corners of her eyes. He would not get her out on that floor gyrating around like a silly schoolgirl. "Matt, one of the first things I told you is that I can't dance. I even demonstrated that to you. So—"

"But, Ran, this ambassador guy has an incredible music library. Looks like he bought out the music stores as a kid and saved all of those old LPs. Dancing to the oldies would be a wonderful diversion."

She wanted to say yes. Thinking about being in Matt's arms while a slow, romantic song pulled them into its spell was enticing, but slow wasn't the way you danced to oldies. If she could specify something he wouldn't be able to find … "If you can find a classical piece suitable for slow dancing, I'll dance to one song with you. An oldy with a beautiful, classical melody."

He met her gaze. "You're on. I'll look for the music now and after dinner, we'll dance."

She turned to walk away, then looked back. "Remember, I said *classical*, as in Bach or Beethoven, not classic rock. Lots of luck. You'd better start thinking about something else we can do, because—"

"Oh, I've got more suggestions, a lot of them."

She stopped and turned around. "Do I need to call Wes or Cody?"

"That remains to be seen."

"See you at dinner, Matt."

After dinner Randi sat in the great room with Matt, letting dinner settle and letting her mouth cool from the spicy takeout Cody had brought them.

Through the large window they could see the sun touching the horizon. In another fifteen minutes, it moved toward the northwest, gradually sinking behind the Cascade Mountains. The long period of twilight began.

The panorama displayed from the sofa included part of the lake, the mountains beyond it, and a sizeable swatch of azure sky. With the sun gone, the moon had become a yellow crescent in the western sky.

Matt took her hand and gave her a coy smile. "I found your music."

"No way."

His grin morphed to a smile. Matt stood and tugged on her hand.

"Who's the artist?"

"Beethoven."

People didn't dance to Beethoven. "What? Oldies doesn't mean the 1850s and 1860s."

"This is 20th-century music. But it's not *just* Beethoven. Billy Joel re-arranged it a bit."

"You're only saying that to get me to dance with you."

"Ran ... just start dancing and if by ninety seconds into it you aren't convinced, you can beat me to death with a couch pillow."

"It's a deal. But you have to stand still while I whack you. I struck out when I had to chase you."

"Listen to the song first."

She sighed. "All right." Randi stood and walked to the center of the room while Matt fiddled with buttons on the stereo.

"In honor of this beautiful night and my beautiful companion, here's the Beethoven and Billy Joel song, *This Night*." He pushed the button and hurried to reach her before the music started.

She put her arms out in the proper, traditional dancing position.

Matt ignored her arms, slipped in close, and pulled her into a comfortable embrace. "This is a slow dance not a waltz."

The music started, and the melody was enticing. Matt soon had her swaying gently and slowly on the dance floor.

"Nice lyrics, but where's the Beethoven? You've only got ninety seconds."

But soon the romantic melody drew Randi in. She rested her cheek against Matt's neck as they turned on the dance floor.

The moon hung in the western sky and its brilliant yellow reflected in the lake.

Romantic setting? That was an understatement.

The music quickly transitioned to the chorus. A full, rich rendition of a Beethoven sonata, complete with romantic lyrics, filled the great room.

Matt nudged her and again they moved with the melody.

Randi became lost in the music, lost in Matt. And she lost her chance at beating him with a pillow. But pounding him with a pillow wasn't what she wanted. Not now.

Matt held her close. Secure in his arms, swaying to the beautiful melody while the moon shone through the big window, she wished the moment and the song would never end.

When the last measure faded away, the first verse of the song began again. She pulled her head back to look into Matt's eyes. The rapidly fading twilight turned his blue eyes into dark purple inviting pools. There were no lights on in the room, only the moon.

"Our song is playing again," she whispered into his ear. Our song? Why had she—

"I put the track on repeat."

"I said only one song, so you tricked me. But I don't mind doing this one more time." She smiled at him.

"It will repeat until we stop it."

"Who wants to stop it?" Randi buried her face in his neck and danced with only Matt and the music on her mind. So what if she couldn't dance well. He had called her beautiful. Why should she care about how her dancing looked to anyone?

Occasionally Matt pressed a soft kiss on her forehead.

Time passed. Wonderful time, but she hadn't a clue how long they'd been dancing.

"Knock, knock, you two." Wes's voice. "Cody said if he heard that Billy Joel song one more time he'd blow the stereo away with his automatic ... or go stir crazy. I couldn't let that happen. He's my partner."

Lights shattered the semi darkness. She squinted from their bright glare and looked toward the entryway, where Wes stood, hands on hips.

Matt hooked her waist with one hand and pulled her beside him, facing Wes.

She gave Wes a mock frown. "Who appointed *you* to be our chaperone?"

"Peterson. From the looks of things, you two need one. Sorry, but it's time to pull the plug on your dance party before Cody starts howling at the moon." Wes turned the lights off. "Having this room lit up like a stage while you two are here doesn't seem like a good idea."

Matt looked at her and smiled, then glanced at Wes." So Cody doesn't like Billy Joel."

"He likes Billy Joel ... in moderation. It's 10:30, how long did you intend to let that song repeat?"

10:30? "Matt, we started an hour and a half ago."

Matt jogged to the stereo and turned it off. "I guess we did get a little carried away."

"Then it's a good thing I showed up," Wes said.

"Thanks, Wes." Randi waved goodbye to him. "You can leave. You've done your duty. Matt and I need to talk."

"Is everything okay?" Wes's voice grew serious.

She laughed. "Everything is fine. You're taking good care of us."

"Don't stay here all night. I'm going to check on you and—"

"Goodnight, Wes." She waved again and Wes disappeared from the doorway.

Randi led Matt to the sofa. "And I thought Peterson was the fatherly type."

He sat down beside her. "Wes is a good guy. Now, what do we need to talk about? I hope I didn't—"

"You didn't. That was the most wonderful evening of my life." She gave him a nervous smile. "But I want you to know some things about me."

"Okay. I'm all for unraveling your mysteries."

"Some of the things we've done and said to each other since we met ... they're firsts for me. I've never handed my heart to any other man, not like I offered it to you. You could say I've never kissed any other man, only the boy in high school who stole a kiss by tricking me. I've never danced close, not like we did tonight."

"Ran, I know you are a good person. You don't have to tell me all—"

"But I wanted you to know because, when we first met, I felt like I was throwing myself at you over and over again, and I thought you might think that—"

"It didn't feel anything but good and right to me. I was the one who was doing the wrong things. If I'd been open and honest with you from the start, there would have been no misunderstandings."

"It's okay, Matt. Someone was watching out for us." She paused. "And how are things going between you and that Someone?"

"Much better. I stopped looking at my own character and started studying His. You know, He runs to meet returning prodigals. It's who He is. I must've forgotten that somewhere in the far country."

Everything had been building toward this moment since she stepped onto the dance floor with him. Matt's revelation had removed the last remaining barrier between them.

Randi reached for Matt and looked up into his eyes.

Matt stopped her, putting his fingers on her lips.

She didn't understand. Surely he wouldn't walk away again.

He smiled. "Ran, I'm the quarterback. May I call this play?"

Their lips met, ending Matt's words. So who initiated the kiss? Her question lost its importance as the kiss concentrated all the emotions of a romantic evening into a few sweet seconds.

"Matt," she whispered. "Did you plan this whole thing? The music, the dancing ..."

He laid his head on hers. "If I could plan something like this, I would've done it before now." He stood, took her hands, and pulled her to her feet. "I love you, Ran."

She held him and felt his arms wrap snugly around her. "I love you too, sweetheart. Goodnight."

When Randi crawled into bed at 11:30, sleep was a distant place reachable only by a long journey through her mind and her heart. Her mind was filled with Matt, filled with memories of emotions and sensations he created and with those wonderful, mesmerizing ninety minutes on the dance floor with him.

No matter what Cody thought about it, that song would be Matt's and hers for the rest of their lives. Randi prayed their life together would be long, not one cut short by a drug cartel's assassin.

Chapter 23

June 2, 2:00 AM

It was game time. Zambada drove south on Highway 971 from the Bear Creek Cabins toward Chelan. When he reached Highway 97, he pulled into a dirt parking area, cut the lights, the engine, and pulled out his cell.

Earlier in the day, Bennie had brought his most powerful laptop from Wenatchee. He left it at the cabin and then headed back to Wenatchee with his other laptop, which had also been configured to access the security system at the safe house.

Bennie was good at what he did, but it was Zambada's life on the line, and he would walk Bennie through his checklist one more time, including Bennie's Skype hack, before approaching the safe house.

At 2:30 a.m., Zambada placed a call to Bennie. "Are you ready to start the video feed?"

"When you give me go-ahead, I start video two minutes after."

"Then I will call again two minutes before I enter camera range. What about Luis's laptop? Did you test the hacked version of Skype?"

"Of course, I check eet, Zambo. We can make phone call or start Skype video session from cabin and it pass through Luis's machine at motel. Marshals will never know we running our show from Bear Creek Cabins."

If the pudgy programmer-analyst was wrong about the Skype pass through, he would be paid ... with a magazine full of lead. "How soon can Luis and Teo leave the motel in Chelan?"

"Once we place first call to safe house, if things work okay, Luis and Teo can forget about computer and get ready for target practice on Matt Mathison."

"But can they tell if their computer has been detected while it's running a Skype session?"

"Sure. Luis is that good. Not much better though, so you must not think Luis can replace Bennie."

"You pull this off, and your job is secure, Bennie. When you leave the motel, the minute you reach Bear Creek, let me know if you see any signs that the marshals know Randi Richards is gone."

If he was a religious man, he would pray it was Barbie in the room he entered. Reason number one—packing two-hundred-twenty-five-pound Matt Mathison for two hundred and fifty yards to his car would be more than exhausting. Reason number two—if it was Matt in the bedroom, applying the sleeper hold on him might be difficult. If Zambada didn't catch Mathison by complete surprise, it might be impossible.

"What else you want, Zambo?"

"Once they discover one of their witnesses is missing, we'll make our first call to them as soon as possible. The less time we allow them to prepare, the better. So stay on top of events at the safe house. Let me know if you see any signs that they know I've been there."

"If I see, I call Zambo right then."

"But, Bennie, I want to be at the cabin when we place our first call to them. So wait for me."

"Bennie will get Skype ready to go and wait for you."

It would take fifteen minutes to move the girl to his car and twenty-five more to get to the cabin. Zambada couldn't afford delays or the risk of being found would grow. "Are you sure you can carry out our plan without any hitches?"

"I understand. But this ees *third time* we go over plan. Bennie is no dummy like Luis. He just hide behind his machine and—"

"Enough about Luis. He has a role and he'll perform it. I'm headed toward the safe house now. I'll call you in about thirty minutes. That's when you hijack the video feed."

Zambada closed his cell and turned onto Highway 97 toward Chelan, and beyond that, the safe house.

* * *

At 1:00 a.m. Randi's mind was still too filled with thoughts and emotions to sleep. She felt like a silly schoolgirl crazy with puppy love. But her feelings for Matt were far more than a schoolgirl crush. This was a man she could spend her entire life with and be happier than she had ever imagined.

A knock sounded on her bedroom door. That was strange. The marshals had never woken her when they made their rounds. This late, it must be either Jake or Andy. They normally worked the night shift.

The knock sounded again.

"Who is it?"

"It's Matt."

"What are you doing knocking on my door at one o'clock?" She got up, walked to the door, and opened it. "Besides, my room is off limits. Remember?"

Matt's gaze darted around the room as if trying to see everything at once. It finally focused on her. "I got worried about you. I dozed, had a bad dream, then woke up. I'm sorry, Ran. But I needed to know you were safe."

"I'm fine. But you'd better get back to your room before the night shift catches us together." She grinned. "They might tell Wes or Peterson."

She pulled Matt's head toward hers, turned his head, and softly kissed his cheek. When she glanced into his eyes, the warmth told her she had gotten the message across to him. She would've liked a lot more, but it wouldn't be appropriate. And it would be tempting ... far too tempting. "Goodnight, Matt."

"Good night, sweetheart." Matt headed back to his own room.

She smiled as she slipped under the covers. They had both used the term of endearment today, a word that made them sound like a married couple. That seemed to be where they were headed.

Randi sighed and allowed the pleasant thoughts to drift through her mind until it rested in a place of peace.

* * *

At 2:45 a.m., Zambada turned onto Boyd Road and drove slowly up the steep hill until he reached a wide dirt driveway leading to an equipment storage building. He turned off his headlights and rolled quietly behind the windbreak shielding the building from the strong southerly winds.

There were no signs that he had attracted any attention, so he climbed out of his car, unlocked the trunk, but left it down. Diagonally up the hill, on top of a bluff, the safe house lay two hundred and fifty yards away.

He strapped on his tool belt, containing various tools, the biggest of which was the silent drill.

Zambada's path was dotted with sagebrush which gave way to tumbleweeds extending to the base of the bluff. The last forty feet up to the house was steep.

Zambada stopped, turned his phone volume down, and placed a call to Bennie. "Tell me when you've got the feed going."

In a couple of minutes Bennie whispered over the phone, "Feed ees running. Looks perfecto."

He closed his cell and pulled out the silent drill. Zambada was attached to this efficient tool that could drill quickly and almost silently through glass. It came from a reseller in Colombia, because the manufacturer in the UK only dealt with the military and law enforcement. If Barbie was cooperative, he would not have to leave his drill behind.

As Zambada climbed the bluff to reach the point where the security system would have normally picked him up, he laughed quietly. Westminster developed the silent drill for use by law enforcement and intelligence agencies against people like him. Then they wouldn't sell him one. So tonight he would turn the tables.

He stopped when the camera Bennie had blocked came into view. It should now be sending last night's video.

No movement. Nothing unusual came from the house.

He crouched and inched ahead. When he reached the edge of the lawn, he crawled to the side of the house. Zambada rose to his feet, took his dim light, and shined it downward through the window at the latch. The peg at the bottom was up, out of the slot, but the lever was down and locked.

He quickly set up the drill on the glass above the lock and bored slowly, almost silently, until the small drill bit slid through the window. After slipping in his wire, he pulled the lever, unlocking the window, and used the wire to push back the drapes and peer in.

The red face of a digital clock lit the room enough to see Randi Richards asleep in her bed. He had guessed correctly.

The bed sat against an adjacent wall. Good. No furniture under the window to restrict him.

Zambada greased the groove and slid the window open.

The moon had disappeared over the horizon an hour ago, so he had little fear of being seen as he climbed through the window in his black attire. His gaze remained locked on the girl who, even with her features dimly lit by the red light, clearly outshone any man's perception of the doll she resembled.

* * *

Randi's dream morphed to a scene where an arm slid around her head. It brushed against her hair. Was Matt in the room? "Matt, you shouldn't—" her mouth stuck shut. Tape! She tried to yell, but the sound was muted, trapped in her throat.

The arm tightened around her neck, clamping both sides like a vice.

She kicked, jabbed, and elbowed her assailant.

He was strong, but so was she.

Randi pounded on the wall, but he rolled her to the center of the bed and wrapped his leg around hers like a grapevine. All the time his arm squeezed her neck until her head buzzed. Her strength flowed out of her muscles as the gray fuzziness invaded her mind and then darkened to black.

* * *

Zambada felt the girl go limp. He kept a tight squeeze on her neck with one arm and pulled the carefully measured dose of the anesthetic dissolved in DMSO from a pouch on his belt. He swabbed it on her upper arms and neck, hoping the information he got about the absorption rate and the dosage was correct.

After thirty more seconds, he eased up on the pressure, but kept his arm in place to see if the anesthetic would keep her knocked out. If it worked, she would be out for at least thirty minutes.

She stirred slightly at forty seconds, then quieted. She was breathing, a bit shallow, but enough to stay alive. He carried her to the window and lowered her body to the ground.

The girl was heavy. For a slender girl, too heavy. Probably all the muscle, muscle that had nearly overpowered him at one point in the struggle. It was embarrassing, but it no longer mattered.

He grabbed his drill, slung the girl over his shoulder in a fireman's carry, and stepped over the bank.

Zambada half walked and half slid to the bottom of the bluff while he balanced the girl on his shoulders. At the bottom, he cut diagonally down the hill toward his car, breathing heavily with his burden.

In his hurry to get away, he pushed himself to his limits. If a marshal checked the room in the next minute or so, his situation could change in an instant, forcing him to kill the girl and run to save his life.

In a few minutes, Zambada reached his car. He nudged the unlocked trunk upward.

It opened.

He dumped the girl inside then grabbed his roll of duct tape. When he finished adding another strip of tape to her mouth, he began working on her hands and feet.

After locking the trunk, he slid into the driver's seat and drove away without turning on his headlights. He let the vehicle idle down the hill in low gear to avoid using his brakes. At the highway, he stopped and studied the house.

No lights that he could see. Nothing to indicate he had been detected.

He turned left onto the highway, hit the headlights, and headed toward the cabin.

In a few minutes, he would call Mr. Mathison. After Matt heard what would happen to Barbie if he didn't surrender, the traitor would comply. Zambada had found that the threat of horrific torture was usually more effective than torture itself.

He hoped that would be the case, because it would be a shame to disfigure such a beautiful woman.

Chapter 24

I love you, Ran. You are so beautiful.

Matt's dream replayed their evening together. But something wasn't right. The dream ended with the sound of running feet. Not Randi's feet.

Heavy feet clomped down the hall.

"She's gone! Her window's unlocked!" Andy's voice came from the hallway.

Wide awake now, Matt sat up on the edge of his bed. The clock said 4:05 a.m. When the words, "she's gone," registered, Matt's heart exploded into a wild drumming in his chest.

By the time he flung his door open, his stomach had become one big knot and threatened to empty its contents.

Matt ran to Randi's door. It stood open. He jumped into her room.

Andy grabbed him and pulled him back into the hallway.

Matt whirled, hands clenched, ready to release his anger and frustration on Andy's face. "Your job was to keep her safe." His words came from somewhere beyond his control. "You incompetent—"

The pain on Andy's face stopped Matt's words. Only a sharp blast of air came out of his mouth.

"You can't go in there, Matt. I can't let you contaminate the evidence."

Down the hallway, from the direction of the great room, Jake trotted their way. Footsteps pounded down the stairway. Probably Wes and Cody.

Contaminate the evidence? The only evidence that mattered to him was the empty bed. Randi was gone and Matt knew who had her. Only a man like Zambada could breach the safe house.

Wes ran down the hallway toward them, the tail of his unbuttoned shirt waving behind him. He stopped near Andy. "Who saw her last?"

Wes's question yanked Matt's mind back to the hallway where now all four marshals huddled.

"I saw her in her room at 1:00 a.m." No one questioned why Matt had looked in her room.

Andy sighed sharply. "I checked on her at 2:30. Everything was fine."

"I'll call Peterson and tell him she disappeared around 3:00 a.m." Cody turned toward the stairway leading up to the marshal's office.

"Okay." Wes faced Andy and Jake. "You two look over my shoulder and take mental notes. I'm going to check the room without disturbing anything the crime-scene crew will need to examine. We'll pass the details to Peterson in a couple of minutes. Jake, you—"

"Wes, it's got to be the video feed." Jake stared down the hallway. "I monitored *that* camera, and the others, nonstop from midnight until just now. No one approached that side of the house. I need Andy for a minute to validate my theory."

"Andy, go with Jake," Wes said. "I'll take the room. In two minutes, we meet in the office and talk to Peterson. Any questions?"

Heads shook.

"Let's go then. Every minute is precious, guys."

Matt stared at the men as they broke from the huddle to execute Wes's instructions. Precious. Every moment he had with Randi was more than precious. Would there be any more moments with her?

The question produced an ache somewhere deep inside, an ache more intense than the pain of Matt's old injuries. He couldn't afford to let his emotions get in the way. Matt needed to control himself as he had many times on a wild, desperate drive to the end zone with time running out.

He was a quarterback, trained for these pressure-packed situations, but what play could he call? There wasn't anything in his playbook for this.

But Matt knew Zambada better than any of the marshals or the FBI. Zambada wanted Matt much more than Randi, and he would use her to get to Matt. Maybe he could use that motive to keep Randi alive. Regardless of what Peterson said in the coming phone call, Matt would try negotiating for her life even if it cost him his.

He turned and ran down the hallway toward the stairs that led up to the office.

* * *

An awareness of her body being jostled about awakened Randi. She tried to think, but her fuzzy mind refused to cooperate.

Hands, arms, feet, legs—her body wouldn't obey her commands. Was she still asleep or in that paralyzed state, the shadowlands between waking and sleeping?

She tried to sit up. Her head smashed into something in the total darkness enveloping her. The bump brought more clarity to her mind.

The man in her room. She needed to fight him off, but where—the tape on her mouth and hands told the story. The dark clad man had won the struggle and had drugged her. But how had he gotten into the safe house and back out again?

Another bump told her another bit of the story. She was bound and gagged with tape and lying in the trunk of a car.

Bound and locked in the trunk of a car!

She couldn't breathe here! Not enough oxygen. She needed to breathe through her mouth.

Randi's stomach quivered until her entire body shook. She was going to smother. With that thought, sanity fled. Nothing mattered but getting free

Randi rolled and kicked. Without shoes, she only smashed her toes. Pain, but no progress.

She screamed, but the muted sound waves only echoed back into her throat, choking her.

The vehicle jerked to a stop.

Rationality returned. With it came the thought of what the car stopping might mean.

She exerted all of her will to be still and listen. If this is where the man planned to kill her, she wouldn't make it easy for him.

No. Killing her wouldn't happen, yet. They would probably use her to get to Matt.

The car door opened. Feet trudged in gravel somewhere outside.

A click sounded near her head, and the trunk lid rose a few inches.

Randi needed to know where she was. If the man moved her from the trunk, she must remember everything about her surroundings.

Slowly the trunk lid rose. A piercing light stabbed her eyes.

"So, you're awake and you don't like the trunk. Out for thirty minutes. The doctor was right on the money with the anesthetic."

She turned her head to avoid the harsh light, but she wanted to see the man. When she glanced at him again, the light was too bright to see his face.

"Do not worry. You will see me soon enough, Barbie."

The named turned embers from long ago into a roaring fire. She pulled her knees to her chest and kicked both feet into the man's chest.

He flew backward out of sight.

Randi rolled to a sitting position.

The man bounced up and glared at her. "If you give me too much trouble, your value to me becomes nothing. I will kill you, and I will do it slowly. Do you understand?"

She had to control her anger. A man who could circumvent the security of the safe house could do things she couldn't imagine, things she didn't want to imagine.

Matt? Was he okay? Of course he was. Or she would be dead. They were using her to lure Matt, and then this monster would kill them both.

"Barbie, your eyes bother me. Oh, they are beautiful, but so hostile. Change that look, or maybe I will put them out, perhaps with acid. I hear it's good for the complexion."

She gasped, and then sought to control her emotions. This man was playing head games with her, like some of the international runners before a race. She had to stare him down and not give in to the fear he tried to instill.

The man suddenly grabbed her, and with incredible strength for a medium-sized man, slung her over his shoulder.

Fighting him now with her hands and feet bound would be pointless. She must bide her time and be ready for any opportunity that came.

The man's heavy steps crunched on gravel, then thumped on wood before he carried her through a doorway. Inside a room, he dropped her on a bed. "I think perhaps we should call Matt Mathison now."

Chapter 25

Bound hand and foot on the bed, Randi studied the wiry man standing on the far side of the room. This had to be the assassin, Zambada. He was the man who approached her when she was launching the radiosonde.

A rotund man, apparently Zambada's partner, sat at a desk typing on a laptop. Probably the cartel's hacker.

"Bennie, did Luis call you when they noticed the girl was gone?"

"Yes. Just before you carry her in."

"And you reminded them that plan B was in effect?"

"Bennie is no fool, Zambo. Luis and Teo are waiting in motel across street from our Skype-relay laptop. So we call Matt now ... tell him to come get his Barbie doll?"

"Things went almost too smoothly. We're ahead of schedule. Let's wait until it's light outside. They need to be able to see Matt in order to take him out from one hundred yards away. We'll wait until six o'clock. When Matt surrenders, it will be at least 6:30 and light enough for the snipers to do their job."

Randi prayed Matt would not agree to surrender to these killers. But her heart told her the truth. Matt would agree for her sake, and the snipers would kill him before any promised exchange ever took place. But first, Matt would want proof that she was alive. What kind of proof?

She needed a plan to warn him. If she could determine where she was, and had the opportunity, she could shout out their location. If she did, Zambada would carry out his threats to kill her. But if it would save Matt ...

* * *

Matt followed the four marshals up the stairway. When he entered the office, Wes already held his cell phone to his ear.

"He's not answering." Wes frowned and ended the call. "I'll give him a few seconds to wake up." He redialed in a few seconds and put his cell on speakerphone.

"Peterson here."

Relief erased the tight lines on Wes's face. "This is Wes Smith. Bad news. They breached the safe house and took Randi."

"What?" Peterson spat out a harsh expletive.

Cody ducked when the word flew across the room. "I've never heard pure-mouth Peterson talk like that."

"Collect all the evidence you can about how they did it. Be prepared to brief me when I arrive. Ruska and I will be there by 6:00 a.m. and I'll have a SWAT team there a short time later. At some point they'll call, wanting to talk to Matt. I want to be there when that call comes in."

At 4:20 a.m., Wes dropped his cell into its holder.

It seemed to Matt that every eye in the room had focused on him.

"Peterson wants a briefing and we don't have much to tell him," Wes said. "Matt, tell us who you think took her."

Matt scanned their faces, then began. "There's only one person in that cartel who could get in here and escape with Randi. We already know he's in the area ... Zambada."

Wes tucked a loose tail of his shirt in and looked up at Matt. "You briefed Peterson on Zambada while you were in Forks. Is there anything you forgot to mention?"

Matt met Wes's gaze. "The guy's resume has a skill list that goes on for pages. I didn't give them an exhaustive list of what he can do."

"Then you need to tell us everything you know about this guy." Wes stood with folded arms, waiting.

Over the next few minutes, Matt told them some of the skills the cartel attributed to Zambada and emphasized that the assassin reported directly to the leader, Arellano.

When Matt finished, Wes took a deep breath and exhaled. "Sounds like we're up against a world-class, jack-of-all-trades killer."

"We didn't have time to check all the cameras and the video feeds," Jake said.

"Okay, Jake, you watch the video feeds," Wes said. "I'm going to walk around the house, then the interior hallways. Any feeds that I don't show up in are still hijacked. Andy, check the bedroom again for anything we overlooked, but leave everything intact for the crime scene crew. Let's meet back here in ten minutes. 4:40 a.m." Wes paused and shook his head. "Guys, we need a plan and the evidence to support it before Peterson arrives, or it's going to get doggoned unpleasant. We have never lost anyone we've protected, and we're not going to lose Randi. Whatever it takes to get her back, we'll do it. Let's go."

Matt sat across the desktop from Jake, while he stared at the monitor. Zambada had obviously planned well. They would never be able to get to Randi without the assassin killing her. Only one Person could help them in this situation. Matt rested his head in his hands and pled with Him for Randi's life.

After his desperate prayer ended, Matt's mind continued working on a plan to solve what seemed to be an intractable problem. When feet clomped up the stairway, his plan remained as it had started, empty.

Wes entered first. "What did you see, Jake?"

"The video feed from the camera outside, near Randi's room, is still showing bogus video. The others are all okay."

Andy and Cody stepped into the room and stopped beside Wes. "Did you two hear Jake?"

"Yeah," Andy said.

Cody nodded.

"That fits this whole scenario." Wes shook his head. "As bad as it is, we know Randi is alive and probably unharmed.

They need her to get to Matt." He sighed. "At least we have something to tell Peterson. What else did you find?"

"Did you guys smell anything when you first went into Randi's room?" Andy scanned the other men's faces.

No replies.

"How about a sickening, sweet garlic smell?" Andy looked at everyone in the room again. "Did any of you smell it when you first entered Randi's room?"

"Yeah, I think I did." Jake said. "Chloroform maybe?"

Wes nodded and stared across the room. "Now that I think about it, I smelled something too. Funny what you miss when something else has your attention. Probably because I smelled a rat."

Cody cleared his throat. "The rat drilled through the window and left some things behind that the CS people will want to examine."

"That's the way it always goes." Wes shook his head. "He probably used a silent drill, the one the Brits promised us they wouldn't sell to the bad guys."

Jake gave Wes a serious frown. "But aren't those distributed to several countries?"

"Like any technology or weapons, if you've got enough money, you can buy it," Cody said.

Matt sat up in his chair. "These guys have enough money to buy anything they want, except maybe a nuclear bomb."

Cody shoved his hands in his pockets. "One greedy Russian could change that."

Andy frowned at Cody. "We need to get focused here. Let's talk about how we solve *our* problem."

Matt needed help. He needed hope, and he wasn't getting any of that here. His stomach threatened to erupt any moment.

If God really was in control, Matt needed a reminder. He rose from his chair. "I'm going back to my room until

Peterson arrives. I'll come back up when I hear the chopper."

Wes placed a firm hand on Matt's shoulder. "Not a good idea. I want you right here, Matt, where we can see you. It's only a few minutes until Pete gets here, anyway. And, Matt, if your phone rings, we *all* need to hear the conversation."

Matt sat back down. He could pray silently here as well as in his room. But this didn't seem to be a time for silent prayer, the kind you do while you're sitting in a chair. He needed to be on his knees or on his face pouring out the agony in his heart to the only One who had the power to save Randi Richards.

Chapter 26

Matt glanced at the wall clock when he heard the helicopter. 5:50 a.m. Peterson was late, but then it was hardly more than an hour and a half since they rousted him out of bed.

The marshals were good people, but Peterson instilled a confidence Matt needed now. Despite the many prayers he'd launched over the previous twenty-five minutes, sometimes people needed something tangible, something to happen, some person to come on the scene. He hoped God understood Matt's weakness.

A thought struck him. Maybe Peterson was the answer to his prayers ... or at least part of the answer.

Before his musings ended, the front door to the house opened and closed. A helicopter rotor was still spinning down when footsteps sounded on the stairway.

Peterson's big frame filled the doorway. "Don't give me excuses. We don't have the time." He focused on Wes. "Just tell me how he got in. Most important things first."

"First, they hijacked the video feed from one of our cameras and fed us bogus video. The man—we think it was Zambada—drilled through the glass of her bedroom window, unlocked it, and got in. Somehow he quietly disabled Randi—"

"Quietly disabled? How could he have quietly disabled her? He would have had to render her unconscious. She's a tough girl, and strong." Peterson paused and stared across the room at the wall.

"We were just talking about that." Wes shifted his feet and shook his head. "We don't know what it was, but her room reeked of garlic ... sweet garlic. It wasn't chloroform, but..."

Peterson rubbed his chin and turned to Ruska. "Sounds like DMSO used as an agent to enhance the absorption of some anesthetic. You rub it on and then keep the person controlled until they go to sleep."

Ruska nodded slowly. "Is the video feed back to normal?"

Jake wiggled the mouse attached to the host computer, and the screen lit. "We sat a bucket on the lawn. Don't see it by the window. It's still hijacked."

"We've got to find out where that feed is coming from. We need Jennifer. ASAP." He turned toward Agent Ruska. "Send a helicopter to pick her up, then get her on the phone for me."

Matt looked up into the tall agent's eyes. "Who's Jennifer?"

Wes smiled. It was the first smile Matt had seen in two hours. "Andy, Jake, you two probably haven't been with the office long enough to hear about her. She's one incredible lady. People at the office nicknamed her Miss Universe."

"Miss Universe?" Jake gave Wes a wild-eyed glare. "Randi's a beautiful young woman, but I've got news for you, Wes. This ain't no beauty pageant."

Peterson cleared his throat while Ruska punched in a number on his cell. "She's married, guys, so wipe that silly look off your face, Cody. Jennifer's an NSA employee. The world's leading Internet forensics expert. She's five foot two and about one-hundred-ten pounds of dynamite. If you value your head, don't call her Miss Universe. She hates that label. Her grandfather holds a sixth-degree black belt in Karate, and he taught her well."

Ruska handed Peterson his phone. "Here she is, but it doesn't sound too promising."

"You all need to be in on this." Peterson turned on the speakerphone.

Something that sounded like retching came through the speaker, followed by a splash, a moan, and the sound of a flushing toilet.

"Jennifer, this is Peterson. Are you okay?"

"No." A woman's alto voice came from the phone, followed by another retch and a flush of the toilet. "Oh, Lee, I'm going to kill you for this."

Peterson pursed his lips and waited.

A man's voice sounded in the background. "You're sick, Jen."

"No lie," Jennifer said, then retched again. "You did this to me."

"You're pregnant, honey. That's terrific," the man's voice said.

"If it's terrific, then you carry the baby." She blew a breath into the phone. "I'm sorry, Peterson. Morning sickness like never before."

Peterson shook his head. "I know our timing is really bad, but are you up to a helicopter ride to Chelan and some cyber sleuthing to save a young woman's life?"

"Save her life?" Jennifer breathed out another low moan. "I'll try. What's happening?"

Peterson gave her the thirty-second nutshell version of Randi's situation and a brief description of the hijacked video feed.

"Are we going to be in the Chelan area the whole time?"

"I think so, but that could change."

Jennifer groaned and blew out a breath, creating static over the phone. "Then, I'll bring my C-Sat laptop. It should give me Internet access anywhere in that area. When will the helicopter be arriving?"

"Anytime. It's landing at the middle school ball field a block and a half from your house."

"Gee, thanks for the advance notice. And Peterson ... you owe me big time. Oh, crud!" Another retch came through the speaker, followed by a couple of deep breaths. "I can't believe I was actually thinking about making you this baby's godfather."

"Sweetheart ... bring me the box of kitchen garbage bags, please. And will you slip my laptop into its case? I'll see you in about an hour, Peterson."

"Thanks, Jennifer."

The call ended.

What on earth was Peterson thinking? Matt clamped his hand on the tall man's shoulder. "You heard her. Can she do this? She's puking her guts out."

"Matt, this is one tough little lady we're bringing in to help. Her IQ is off the charts."

"But that's only part of the reason they call her Miss U." Wes said.

Peterson cleared his throat. "Enough with the names. Just pray the video feed continues until she gets here, or we're toast."

Chapter 27

Randi's taped wrists throbbed as she lay on her side crosswise on the bed. In the past two hours, she had tried several times to pray for her and for Matt. At each attempt, her mind drifted off into gray fuzziness. But over the past several minutes, the effects of the anesthesia seemed to be subsiding.

Where was she? The answer to that question could save her life, and possibly Matt's.

Zambada and his hacker, Bennie, had mentioned snipers at another location, a place where they would shoot Matt. They would call him soon, and she needed to be prepared to warn him.

Bennie walked to a window and pushed the heavy curtains aside. "It ees light enough, Zambo."

"Okay. You place the call"

"Remember, we pass our Skype call through Luis's laptop at motel, so there will be small delay before we hear and before they hear. You should speak immediately after they speak, so we give no clue what we are doing."

"I've got it, Bennie. I'm not a fool." Zambada pointed at the computer screen. "Place the call, then sit by Barbie and keep her quiet."

"Matt will want proof that she ees okay. It too risky to let her—"

"I've got it covered. Just show me how to mute the sound and block the video during the call."

While Bennie gave instructions to Zambada, Randi scanned anything within her field of vision that might provide clues about her location.

A pamphlet lay on the stand beside her bed. It appeared to be facedown.

She blinked her eyes, trying to remove the fuzziness from her vision. She strained to focus on the brochure. It *was* face down. Randi glanced back at Zambada and Bennie.

Both were focused on the computer screen.

She scooted to the edge of the bed and nudged the pamphlet with her elbow.

It dropped to the floor, making only a small sound, but one that drew Zambada's gaze.

"If you don't stop wiggling around on that bed. I'll administer something that will stop all of your movement, maybe permanently." His glare faded to a smirk.

She stopped moving but kept her head on the edge of the bed.

"That's more like it." Zambada turned his attention back to Bennie and the computer.

From where her head rested, Randi could look down to the floor. The pamphlet had flipped during its fall. She strained to read the front of the brochure.

The logo at the top consisted of letters—words forming the crude shape of a bear. Her gaze followed the trail of letters, inverting in her mind those that were upside down.

Bear Cabins ... at Ten Mile Creek.

"Place the call, Bennie."

Bennie sat in front of the laptop, clicking and typing, placing a call that would draw Matt into danger.

Randi's urge to intervene grew until she was shaking. Her heart drummed in her chest until she feared they would hear it.

Would they remove the tape so Matt could see she was unharmed? She could yell their location if they removed the tape from her mouth, but would they kill her if she did? What if they only freed her hands? What if they didn't remove any tape? That would only leave her with head motion and her eyes. What could she do with them?

* * *

The tension in the room, as they waited for a phone call, grew unbearable. And Peterson's antsy foot shuffling was getting to Matt.

Peterson sat up in his chair. "Let's go over the ground rules one more time."

"I understand the rules, Peterson. We don't negotiate with terrorists and kidnappers." Matt growled the words, taking his frustration out on the tall FBI agent.

Matt's cell phone rang.

"Quiet, everybody. No noise in the room." Peterson scanned every face in the office.

Matt turned on the speakerphone, as instructed, and answered the call. "Hello."

"Is this my amigo, Matt Mathison?"

"I'm not your friend, Zambada."

"It's okay. I am not insulted. You see, we have someone who is, shall we say, closer than a friend. We have her at the spa and are preparing a facial for her, my patented mud pack. It has a special moisturizer, hydrochloric acid."

Matt's hands balled into tight fists. He clenched his jaw and struggled to keep his composure.

"Is my amigo still there?"

"What do you want from me?"

"We will exchange the Barbie doll for you, and I will skip the mud pack if you turn yourself over to us in forty-five minutes. Be at the Lake View Motel, room number 14, no later than 7:00 a.m."

Zambada had gone straight to his point. Matt couldn't let the phone call end yet. "If you hurt her, you'll never get me. I want to talk to her to make sure she's okay."

Matt felt a sharp poke in his back. He was violating Peterson's guidelines for this call.

He ignored the poke and the guidelines. "You prove to me that she's okay, or it's no deal, Zambo." The anger in Matt's voice grew. He didn't care. Maybe Zambada would realize he must bend or Zambada's proposed deal would break. Could he communicate that without pushing the man over the edge?

"I will consider your request ..."

The line went silent.

"I think he's put me on hold or muted—"

Peterson's index finger made the hush gesture against his lips.

Matt waited.

* * *

Randi listened. She could hear Matt's end of the call through the tinny, bass-challenged speaker on the laptop. The sound of his voice created a growing ache deep inside. Nothing would stop that ache except being with him, feeling his arms around her. If it became clear that it wasn't possible, her choice was clear. She would give her life for his. That would require warning Matt about the sniper. But Zambada might never give her an opportunity.

When the speaker went silent, Zambada whirled in his chair to face Bennie. "It's too risky to let her talk with him. We'll use your suggestion and set up a video session so they can see her."

"As I tell you earlier, if they have Skype, ees no problem. Since we hide behind Luis's machine, there ees no risk if we do this one time only."

"I will give them a few moments to stew. Then they can see the girl, and Matt surrenders or ..." he pointed his finger at her face "... Barbie has a big problem with her complexion."

Zambada turned back to the laptop. "It must be your lucky—"

"I want to see Randi, now."

"Do you have Skype on the computer in your safe house?" Zambada clicked with the mouse and spun his chair toward Bennie.

Zambada must have muted the sound on this end again.

"Zambo, were you, maybe, too much careless with your words?"

"It doesn't matter at this juncture. The marshals know that we have a certain degree of intimacy with the security systems controller. You told me it did not have Skype installed. We can afford one short delay. But Matt might try to stall."

"Thirty minutes, Zambo."

"Trying to impress me, Bennie?"

"No. I know what you want. Give him thirty minutes to do install."

Matt hadn't tried to reply yet. After a few more seconds of silence, his voice returned. "We're using the security system's computer. Some of the original software was uninstalled. Probably for security purposes. We need to re-install Skype."

"You have twenty-five minutes. At 6:50, if you do not answer our Skype call, the fun begins here. All kinds of fun."

Matt's heavy breathing was clearly audible.

Her heart broke for him. No one should be treated this way. Zambada was a monster, an intelligent and cruel one. In that moment, she wanted to kill him. But more likely it would be him who killed her.

"7:30." Matt's voice again. "The distribution disks for the OS aren't here. We have to download Skype and configure it. 6:50 is not possible. And ... how will you place a call to us, you don't know our—"

"We will know." Zambada glanced up at Bennie.

Bennie nodded to him.

"Do not worry. Because you are such a good amigo, Zambada grants your request. But one second past 7:30 and Barbie begins to scream and scream and—"

"Shut up, you—"

The sounds of scuffling came from the other end of the conversation. It was silent in the room for a few seconds. Then Matt's voice returned. "7:30, Zambo. I expect to see Randi unharmed."

Tears streamed down her cheeks. What they had put Matt through was inhuman. Then the thought of being burned with acid caused her stomach to roil, giving her the dry heaves. She couldn't make them stop.

Zambada clicked the mouse, rose, and turned toward Randi. "I am so sorry my conversation with your lover made you sick." He dipped in a deep, eloquent bow. "I did not underestimate you after all. One should never underestimate the power of a beautiful woman. But how long will you remain beautiful? I think not very long."

Chapter 28

Matt shifted his weight from one foot to the other as he watched Cody working on the security system's host computer. He glanced at the wall clock. 6:59. "How long does it take to download and install that software?"

Cody glanced up at him. "We don't have to download it. I lied. And to install it—not nearly as long as we told them. But we need to make sure Skype is working. Wes, get on my laptop. Let's check out the installation."

Peterson stepped beside Cody. "Check it thoroughly. We've pushed Zambada as far as we can without repercussions. What we need now is for Jennifer to get here."

Cody shot Peterson a frown and a glance. "You don't even trust me to install a little software?"

"That's not what I meant. Jennifer can work magic with Internet communications. We need her to find these guys and, rest assured, they're not in room 14 at the Lake View Motel. The only people we'll find there will be hiding nearby with their McMillan rifles."

"You mean the minute I get out of your car at the motel I'm dead?"

"No." Peterson looked up at Matt. "More like the second you get out."

"But what if it's the only way to—"

"Matt, you're not going. We might send a car, but if we do, you won't be in it."

Was that the sound of a chopper?

Cody whirled toward them in the computer chair. "Skype is working fine."

The distant sound of a helicopter grew louder.

Peterson looked up at his partner. "Ruska, they've got plenty of room to land, right?"

"I had Mac move our chopper to the far end of the grass. The pad's open for them."

"Where's Mac now?"

Ruska pointed at the stairs. "Down in the kitchen. Where else?"

"I'm going down to make sure he's ready to fly on a moment's notice, and I'll brief Jennifer as she walks in. You guys get off the host PC. In about sixty seconds, it needs to be all Jennifer's."

Could this Jennifer really do all Peterson was counting on? Could anyone besides God? A thought, like a seed, germinated in Matt's mind. Maybe Jennifer was the answer to his prayers for Randi. "Ruska, have you ever met Jennifer?"

"Yeah." Ruska smiled. "You'll never forget her after you meet her. They say she could give Einstein a run for his money, but she does things on computers Einstein couldn't even imagine."

The chopper's engine wound down and soon the front door of the house opened and closed.

Feet ran up the stairs. In front of Peterson, a short, shapely, stunning Asian beauty stepped into the room.

The woman's gaze locked onto Matt's and he felt as if her intense eyes were reading his soul. "So Randi is your fiancée?"

"It's heading that way. If we get her back."

"I'm Jennifer." She shook his hand, then pulled her hand back to her stomach. "This nausea is—don't mind me. It isn't going to kill me."

Matt winced at the words, kill me.

She studied his face. "Sorry. C'mon, let's get this relationship back on track for a wedding somewhere down the road." She gingerly lowered herself into the chair in front of the security systems host computer. "Somebody show me the hijacked camera."

Cody hurried to her side and pointed out the video showing the side of the house near Randi's room.

She pushed a flash drive into the USB port of the host PC. After the operating system recognized it, she opened it and then double-clicked on a file, bringing up a menu in a large window on the computer.

In a few seconds, Jennifer turned to Peterson. "The SSID of the router feeding this is named West SideMotel01. I looked up its IP address. It's on the northwest side of Wenatchee. How quickly can you get me there?"

"Jennifer, we need to make sure it's safe for you to—"

She slapped the top of the desk. "They won't be there, Peterson. Just get me down there, now!"

The force of her voice and the intensity of her eyes forced Matt to step back. She was a spitfire. A smart spitfire. Deep inside, hope was reborn and growing for the first time since early this morning. Jennifer was making something happen. It was more than Peterson had—no, Peterson had demanded that they bring in Jennifer. Matt was beginning to see why.

She stood and picked up her laptop case. "When does the Skype session start?"

Peterson exhaled sharply. "In about eighteen minutes."

"Darn it. Ten minutes down there, five minutes inside, then ten minutes back … that's twenty-five minutes. Let's get to Wenatchee ASAP and then hurry back. Stall them, Matt. Do whatever you have to. I need to be here for part of that call to track it. But there may be important clues in Wenatchee that will help me do that."

Peterson's voice boomed across the room. "Cody, Andy, you two go with her. Keep her safe. Mac is already headed to the chopper. Tell him to push it to the limits."

Jennifer pulled a map from the printer. "I printed out a satellite map of the motel. Let's go."

Matt's gaze followed her. All his hopes for saving Randi were pinned on the young genius.

Before Jennifer left the room, she turned to Matt, gave him thumbs up, then hurried down the stairs.

The chopper engine had already begun to whine, and the wop, wop began.

In thirty seconds, Peterson yelled up the stairs. "They're off. We've got sixteen minutes before the Skype session." Peterson trotted up the stairway. "Are you ready, Matt?"

He pictured Jennifer's intelligent, caring eyes and her thumbs up to him. "Yeah, I'm ready."

Ready to stall? How could he do that? Unexpectedly, a thought entered his consciousness. This was a bit like preserving clock in the final seconds of a football game, something Matt was a master at doing. He had a strategy. For the specifics, he would have to wing it.

In ten minutes, Cody stood and pointed at the PC. "A Skype call is coming in. It's under the name Amigo."

Matt looked at the call on the screen. "Five minutes early. They're testing us. Probably suspected we lied to them."

Matt drew a deep breath and blew it back out.

Time to start winging it.

Chapter 29

Zambada walked slowly across the room and approached Randi.

She rolled into a sitting position on the bed, expecting the worst.

He stepped closer.

She pulled her legs back to kick him.

He grinned, showing two rows of perfect, white teeth. "It is too early to be so desperate. Matt will want to see you, to know that you are safe ... and you will show him, but with your hands, feet, and mouth taped. You nod when he asks. Don't worry. Yes or no will suffice." He unsheathed a large knife from his belt. "And that is all, or I will disfigure you in front of his eyes. Do you understand?"

Randi nodded, trying to avoid focusing on the knife six inches in front of her face. She was becoming hardened to some of the intimidation, because she knew that's what it was. There would be no acid, no carving her face, nothing but intimidation until after this Skype call they were setting up. Then, all bets would be off.

Zambada scooped her up and sat her in a chair two feet from Bennie's side, out of view of the camera. "Cover the camera lens and place the call, Bennie."

"Zambo, are you sure they will be watching host computer?"

"You think everyone is stupid, Bennie. That comes from your own moronic mind and inflated ego. They'll be watching."

"Someday maybe Bennie will no longer do what you say if you keep insulting him."

"I pay you for your work, or I kill you if you won't do it ... or don't do it right. You will do what I say because of our understanding. Now place the call!"

Zambada seemed to lose control whenever Bennie threatened disobedience. She filed it away for future reference, and prepared to communicate with Matt. But how?

* * *

Matt sat beside Cody as he clicked to accept the call.

"Slide in front of the camera, Matt," Cody said. "You've got it now. Just remember what we told you."

Peterson's phone rang. "Doggone it. Bad timing. It's Jennifer. I've got to take it." He stepped out of the room.

Jennifer might have relevant information that would impact their strategy, maybe Randi's safety. He took the mouse and looked into the webcam.

"Can my amigo hear me?" Zambada's voice.

Matt clicked the disconnect icon.

Skype dropped the call.

Cody glared at him. "What the—"

"Peterson," Matt yelled. "I'm off the call for a minute or so. What did Jennifer find out? Should we change our strategy?"

Peterson's big frame filled the doorway, and he was also glaring at Matt. "Do you *ever* follow directions?"

"Didn't like the defense, so I called an audible. What does Jennifer say I should do?" A small window popped open on the screen.

"So, she won you over too." Peterson shook his head. "The helicopter is headed back. Pick up the call when they call back and—"

"They're calling back now."

"Tell them you'll surrender to them, but you need to see that Randi is safe immediately before you surrender. Jennifer said to tell them to Skype her laptop at this address." Peterson handed him a slip of paper.

"They'll be suspicious. Where shall I say this laptop appeared from? We only had a Skype-less PC a few minutes ago."

"Say you'll Skype from your laptop at a Wi-Fi hotspot in Chelan, near the motel, and that you'll surrender to them two minutes after you see that Randi is okay. And, Matt, demand forty more minutes before the final Skype call."

"So now we're Skyping from my laptop? And forty minutes? I hope you have a good excuse in mind for the delay. Isn't it only ten minutes to Chelan from here?"

"Tell them it will take a few minutes to arrange a ride, and your ride is bringing you a laptop. Jennifer will be here in less than ten. Got all that?"

"I think so."

"You don't surrender to them before ..." Peterson rubbed his chin, obviously calculating the latest possible time that might work. "8:30. Not before 8:30."

Matt took a deep breath and tried to concentrate. With so much on the line, he shot up a prayer. This time he had confidence that it went above the ceiling. God was back in his life, despite everything he had done. But that didn't automatically guarantee Randi's safety.

He clicked the icon and looked into the webcam. "Sorry. We had problems."

"Your tall, perfect Barbie doll had problems too."

He couldn't see Zambada. They had covered the webcam on their end.

"If you hurt her, the deal is off."

"Zambo never hurts anyone who does not deserve it."

"You just incriminated yourself, Zambo. You gave us your name."

Immediately, the tone of his voice changed to the icy killer Matt remembered. "Let's cut to the chase. I will show you Randi. You ask her a yes-or-no question. She nods her reply and—"

"No, Zambo. I ask her two questions and I get two responses. I don't want you feeding us bogus video again."

"Two questions then," Zambada growled at him. "Do it now."

Randi's tape-covered face appeared in the Skype window.

He maximized it to see more detail. "I love you, Ran. Are you okay?"

She blinked her eyes several times, became still, then nodded.

He glanced at Peterson.

He nodded to Matt.

"Second question ..."

Randi blinked her eyes again.

Matt counted. Ten blinks. Then he heard the sound of an approaching helicopter.

"Uh ..."

"Finish it now, Matt, or I will kill her in front of you!" Zambada's growl grew to a roar.

"Ran, you need to do whatever they tell you, do you understand?"

She shook her head.

"Wrong answer, Zambada," Matt yelled. "You've dummied the video! This isn't live and Randi might not be either."

Cody jabbed him in the shoulder outside the view of the camera. He had begun improvising, and evidently the coach didn't like the play he had called.

"You'd better do something to prove this isn't pre-recorded, right now, or the deal is off ... all of it."

A hand appeared in the Skype window and ripped the tape from her mouth.

Randi gasped.

Another hand jammed a gun against her head. "Only one question, you ..." A stream of vulgarity blasted from Zambada's ample vocabulary. Those words, screamed into Randi's ear, made Matt wince.

He took a calming breath and focused on Randi. "What's our song, Ran?"

She smiled through a sob. "'This Night' ... and I love you too, Matt."

Randi disappeared.

"How touching." Zambada's calm, mocking voice was back.

"Zambada, I'm not surrendering to you unless I know she's still alright immediately before the exchange. So we'll Skype from a Wi-Fi spot near the motel. Then I'll do the exchange."

"You did not have Skype. Said you had to install it. Where did this laptop magically appear from?" Zambada sneered at him. "I am disappointed in my amigo. You have lied to me all along. We Skype in twenty minutes, or I start killing her ... slowly."

"Zambada, I can't do that. My ride is bringing my laptop, but it's not here yet. It will take a few minutes to get the laptop ready to connect from the Wi-Fi spot. I need forty minutes."

"You can have until 8:20. The clock is ticking. You are using up your time."

"I'll be there at 8:30, Zambada. I can be ready to Skype and see Randi ... by 8:30. If I don't see her then, I'm not going to show."

Zambada spewed another string of words from the dregs of his vocabulary, lapsing into Spanish near the end.

The sound of the front door slamming echoed through the hallway.

"If you come online one second after 8:30, I will peel her alive."

The call ended, and Matt exhaled the tension in a sharp blast of air.

Jennifer rushed into the room carrying two laptops. "The Skype sessions are being passed through another machine they're hiding behind. I'm hoping this laptop I picked up in Wenatchee will give us some clues."

"But how did you—?"

"Don't ask, Matt. I can't tell you." Jennifer placed a laptop beside the host computer.

Matt turned to Cody and Peterson. "You saw those blinks from Randi. She did it ten times. It had to be a clue about her location."

Five minutes later, Jennifer had booted the laptop from Wenatchee and loaded one of her own programs. "We're running out of time. My program might take too long. I'm going to try a shortcut, and gamble that the missing piece is in the event log on this machine." She clicked the mouse a few times and waited. "There's a file buried deep in the event log hierarchy. I'm going to check it. Pray that we'll get lucky."

Matt stepped behind her and watched. She opened the event viewer and went into the Applications and Services Logs. Three levels deeper there was a folder, WLAN-AutoConfig, with an event log named Operational. Jennifer put the mouse cursor on the log. "In there are, among other things, all the Wi-Fi logins. I'm looking for a recent one that's hopefully not from the Wenatchee motel. Maybe they had this machine with them at—okay. Here's a login. Notice that if I look at the properties of the record, the SSID of the router shows up." She scrolled through the properties. "SSID's can be up to thirty-two characters and most motels just use their motel name for the router. See ... bearcabinsat10milecreek01."

"Ten." Matt clamped a hand on Jennifer's shoulder. "Ten blinks. Randi was telling us with her eyes."

"Where is this place?" Peterson said.

She pasted the name into Google maps and pressed enter. "Look. It's only fifteen miles from here. Okay. The map's on its way to the printer ... two copies."

Peterson peered over her shoulder. "We can drive it in twenty-five minutes. But by the time we get out of here it will be nearly 8:10. Matt needs to Skype them at 8:30."

Jennifer glanced up at Peterson. "I knew there would be a good reason to bring my C-Sat laptop. Matt and I will be in the back of your car. I'll hold the laptop and Matt can slide down, so they only see his face from his webcam. We'll Skype until we arrive. Then it's all up to the FBI."

Peterson rubbed his hands together. "Ruska, notify the SWAT team to load up and follow us to the Bear Cabins. I'll direct as we contain and capture. Let's try to surprise them before Randi goes from a captive to a hostage. Cody, back the car up to the front door. Wes, just in case, you guys check the area for snipers before we load up."

Jennifer clamped onto Matt's arm with a surprising strength in her grip. "Matt, she's a beautiful young woman. I prayed for her half the way over here. Are you a praying man?" She peered so intently into his eyes it seemed she was reading his thoughts.

"Yes. I've been praying too."

"Good. Until we place that Skype call, maybe we should both pray."

"Thanks, Jennifer. I'm so nervous that I'm shaking. This isn't anything like a last-minute drive in a football game. My whole life is on the line. Without Randi, I—"

"Without Randi is not an option. Not for us." Jennifer scooped up her laptop. "Let's go."

"All clear." Wes's voice came from the front door.

Peterson motioned toward the door. "Let's lead the SWAT team to that cabin. In the car, you two."

Chapter 30

The tension in the cabin grew thick. It came from Zambada's and Bennie's voices. It filled Randi's mind and her heart. It drove her to prayer. Prayer for the marshals, the FBI. Prayer for Matt. And prayer for her that, somehow, they would find her.

The final call and talk with Matt would begin in only a few minutes. Matt would supposedly surrender to them, though she couldn't believe Peterson would agree to a surrender. She knew Matt would want to. Perhaps he would try to surrender anyway, for her sake.

Last night they had danced, and she had envisioned a future with the strong, magnificent man who loved her. But the coming Skype call might be the last time she saw Matt in this life. The last time she heard his voice.

She looked across the room at the almost likable Bennie and the viper, Zambada. Randi did not want her life to end with only those two for company.

Please make a way for me. Show me what to do.

Zambada stood, turned slowly toward her, and walked her way. "Bennie, in a few minutes Matt will be taken care of. We can take our time when leaving. Perhaps thirty minutes. Would you like ..." He pointed at her.

She met Bennie's gaze from across the room, willing him to leave her alone.

Bennie averted her gaze. "Barbies are not Bennie's type. Too skinny for Bennie." He gave Zambada a toothy grin.

"Bennie is too soft for this job, I think. Maybe I should—"

Bennie's eyes grew wide. "Luis cannot do what I do. Okay." He turned his head toward her, avoiding her eyes. "But now we must focus on call."

* * *

They turned onto 971 and headed toward Bear Creek Road.

"We have seven minutes until Zambada's clock runs out," Peterson said,

Matt looked behind them. The SWAT team's van turned off Highway 97, but a car entering the highway cut in front of them.

Tires screeched. The car hit the van, and a muffled crash sounded from one hundred yards behind them.

"Peterson, that car—"

"I see it. Keep going, Ruska. We're running out of time. I'll call and get their status. But we can't stop." He pulled out his cell and hit a couple of buttons.

"Are you all okay? ... That's good, but what about the van? ... How long will that take? ... Ruska and I will proceed. When you arrive, Ruska and I will have moved in, so come in easy and come in from the east." He closed his cell. "The van's fender is bent against the tire. They're going to pry it out from the tires. But I doubt they will catch up to us before we have to move in. Step on it, Ruska. Contain and capture might take a little longer with only two of us."

With an unlikely car crash in the middle of nowhere, the odds of successfully freeing Randi had just gotten slimmer.

Peterson pushed a small handgun at Jennifer. "Here's my backup. I've seen you in action, so I trust you with it. But you two stay in the car. If you do, you shouldn't need the gun. Do you understand?"

Matt and Jennifer nodded as the car sped up 971 toward the intersection with Bear Creek Road.

In a few minutes, Ruska turned hard left onto Bear Creek Road, throwing Matt and Jennifer to one side.

"It's 8:28." Jennifer called out. "I'm placing the call now."

* * *

Bennie's gaze froze on the laptop. "Ai yai yai!"

Randi raised her head from the bed, studying Bennie's reaction.

"I do not like the sound of that." Zambada turned from Randi and strode toward the laptop.

Bennie pointed at the screen. "Skype connection requested. Call from Matt."

This might be her final attempt to stay alive, or to save Matt. A muddle of thoughts swirled in her head. She had to settle down, watch, and pray for some opportunity.

Zambada's face contorted into a threatening, more evil caricature of itself. "*They* are calling *us*? Tell me this, Bennie. How can *they* call *us*? Does this mean they know where we are?"

"No, Zambo. They might know where Luis's laptop ees. But pass-through hides us from them."

Zambada glared at Bennie. "Skype, hype, hidden behind computers. I do not trust things I cannot see. That is why I hired you. I can see you. Sometime, I think I will kill you, Bennie. And destroy all your computers. You are too sloppy when you work."

Bennie fidgeted, cleared his throat, and avoided Zambada's glare.

If Bennie was worried, this was good news for her, unless Zambada killed them both and ran. But he was too close to getting Matt. Zambada would let this call come through.

"When I hack Skype for pass-through, I did not check to see if call requests from other side come through. It's easy mistake to make when hacking Skype. I did not think they would—"

"Shut up and answer the call!" Zambada continued with a burst of vulgarity that quickly morphed from English to Spanish.

"I pick up call, Zambo. Camera ees covered. You should speak to him now."

* * *

Matt centered his head on the webcam on Jennifer's laptop, filling the display with his face.

Jennifer glanced toward Ruska in the driver's seat. "Can you slow a little and dodge the bumps. We can't let them know we're in a moving car." She moved close to Matt and whispered, "Watch the Skype window on the screen. Make sure your head always fills it."

He nodded and looked at the clock she had opened up on the computer screen. 8:29.

"So, you think you can talk to me whenever you want?" Zambada's voice.

"That's just the way Skype works. I called you back. It's 8:29, Zambo. I couldn't wait any longer, so I tried to—"

"Silence! You should be grateful I did not kill her the moment you called. Are you near the motel?"

Zambada wasn't wasting any time, he was probably getting nervous. "Yes. No more than three minutes away." He glanced at Peterson who pushed a button on his cell, the signal to the SWAT team members who were acting as decoys. They would soon surround the Lake View Motel and hopefully catch the snipers.

"No matter what you do, Zambada, I'm not going to that motel until I know Randi is safe. So, we do this like the previous call. If I'm satisfied Randi is unharmed, then we're set for the exchange and I'll go."

Ruska slowed gradually to a stop.

Peterson pointed at a group of cabins through the trees, two hundred yards ahead.

Ruska and Peterson slipped out of the car. The tall FBI agent raised his index finger. They would make their move in one minute.

Zambada shook his head and released a mirthless laugh. "Amigo, you will go when Zambada says you must go. But now you can play Barbie dolls."

186

Zambada disappeared from the screen. In a few seconds, Randi's legs and her bare feet came on the screen. Her face appeared after Zambada placed her in the chair.

"You have two questions, amigo. Ask them." Zambada jerked the tape from her mouth and once again put a gun to her head.

He had to ask the obvious question. "Are you still okay, Ran?"

"Yes, so far. I love you so much—"

"That's enough love talk from Barbie and Ken." Zambada's growl had returned. "Last question."

"We'll dance our song, Ran, just like the title says."

Randi gasped.

He wanted to slip a clue to her, to let her know what was coming. Had he endangered her?

"Yes, we will sweetheart."

Randi fell off the chair and Zambada appeared, glaring at Matt. "I think you are playing other games than Barbie dolls. This call is over. Go to the motel, now!"

"And you'll make the exchange for Randi?"

"Since you play games with me, maybe I will play games with Barbie."

* * *

Zambada closed the Skype session, then scooped her up from the floor and flung her onto the bed.

"Bennie, you check the back and I'll check the front. I did not like the call or Matt's word games. Something's wrong. I can feel it."

A spark of hope lit in her heart and mind. Matt had hinted that he would dance with her *This Night*, the title of their song. But Zambada had suspicions about their coded communication. She needed to be ready for a rescue attempt. She must also steel herself against what Zambada had threatened to do.

"I see no one in back," Bennie said, as he closed the curtains.

Zambada had pulled back a corner of the curtain in the front window. "In the front. Fifty yards out. Someone's moving from tree to tree." Another blast of profanity, this time in Spanish. "You let them find us, Bennie. I would kill you now for your bungling, but I need you. Get your gun. Pull the tape from Barbie's legs. They're strong. Don't let her kick you."

Bennie closed his laptop.

"Forget the stupid computer. Free her legs, now!"

"Okay. Okay." Bennie ripped the tape from Randi's ankles. "But, Zambo, this ees not Bennie's fault. Somehow marshals or FBI must have got world-class hacker. The one who did thees did what ees impossible."

"Enough of your excuses." Zambada grabbed Randi's arms where the tape bound them behind her back and shoved her to the back door. "I hid the car straight ahead through the trees. I'll watch our left. You watch our right. Barbie can be our shield."

Zambada pushed the back door open and shoved Randi out in front of him.

* * *

It looked to Matt like Zambada pushed Randi to the floor as he ended the Skype call. He needed to help her now ... somehow.

Matt opened the rear door of the car. "Sorry, Jennifer. But I've got to go."

"Don't, Matt. You'll interfere with—"

He closed the door, cutting off her words, and sprinted into the trees to his left.

Chapter 31

A large semicircle around the cabins would keep Matt far from the FBI agents. His sprint would put him behind the cabin in about ninety seconds.

Matt ran hard, dodging the pine trees and bushes.

His gut said Zambada would take Randi out the back door. Matt intended to stop them. But he couldn't endanger Randi in the process.

Breathing hard, Matt hid behind a cluster of bushes two hundred yards behind the cabin. He peered through the bushes toward the back door.

Movement between the trees ahead, slightly to his left.

About one-hundred fifty yards from Matt's position, Zambada pushed Randi in front of him, goading her with his gun.

A short, pudgy man trailed them, scanning the forest on their right.

Zambada must've spotted Peterson or Ruska, otherwise they wouldn't be sneaking away with Randi.

Matt turned and scanned the ground for anything he could use as a weapon.

A dry stream bed lay ten yards away. Matt slunk low to the ground and, using the bush as cover, scampered to the rocky area.

Straight ahead, about a hundred yards through the trees, sat a dark-colored vehicle. Probably Zambada's car.

Matt had to stop them before they reached it. He grabbed five rocks and hurried back to the bush.

Less than seventy-five yards away, Zambada pushed Randi with his gun. Bennie walked behind them.

The three were moving directly toward the bush where Matt hid.

He put the rocks on the ground and selected the two largest stones, two to three pounds each.

With Zambada pushing Randi ahead of him, Matt had to let them pass and then attack from behind. He prayed Randi would quickly grasp the situation once he threw the first rock.

Zambada represented a much greater danger than the overweight hacker. Matt would take out Zambo first.

They were only thirty yards away and moving faster now.

Matt had called his play. Now he must execute it with all the skills he had learned as an athlete and the abilities he was blessed with.

Twenty yards away.

Matt trembled from the rush yet welcomed the adrenaline. He needed the strength of an eighty-yard football pass. But this pass had to be complete ... in the end zone. Because shortly after he threw it, come what may, the game would end.

Ten yards away, Zambada goaded Randi by jamming the gun into her back.

She stumbled.

"Move, Barbie, or I will kill you here."

Randi sped up, moving beyond the reach of Zambada's gun.

He lurched to reach her.

When he tried to prod her with the gun, she jumped farther out of his reach.

They passed within five yards of the bush where Matt crouched motionless.

Again, Randi leaped ahead to avoid the gun.

"You red-headed witch, I'll—"

Matt sprang from behind the bush and planted his feet in throwing position.

With the largest rock in his right hand, Matt started his windup. "Zambo! Catch!"

Zambada whirled toward him.

Matt hurled the rock, his right arm cracking like a whip and his hips following through behind the powerful throw.

Zambada locked his gaze on Matt.   By then, the assassin had no time to react.

The three-pound rock hurtled toward the center of his face at nearly one hundred miles per hour.

A loud smack sounded. The force of the rock knocked Zambada from his feet and slammed his back onto the ground.

Bennie finally reacted. His gun hand came up.

Matt launched the other rock and followed through, remaining behind the rock's trajectory, hoping that would shield him, momentarily, from Bennie's gun.

Bennie fired.

The bullet screamed past Matt's left ear.

The stone ricocheted off Bennie's arm, knocking the gun out of his hand and pounding Bennie's chest with a loud thump. Bennie stumbled backward.

Matt charged Bennie.

He accelerated through contact with Bennie's hips, a savage tackle.

Bennie flew backward, smashing into a dead Pine snag.

Matt whirled away from Bennie, trying to find his gun.

Bennie remained against the tree grunting out his pain.

Matt grabbed the gun and trained it on Zambada.

The swarthy assassin lay on his back.

Randi's powerful leg drove her heel deep into Zambada's solar plexus.

His breath rushed from his crushed mouth. He lay writhing on the ground, wheezing like an asthmatic.

Matt jerked back toward Bennie.

He aimed the gun, ready to fire.

Bennie appeared stuck to the tree. Blood dripped onto the base of the snag.

Peterson and Ruska charged through the trees and entered the arena with their guns out.

"What the—" Peterson stopped.

Ruska nearly collided with him.

The tall FBI agent quickly scanned the scene, then lowered his gun. "Mathison, I ought to arrest you for interfering with a police officer."

Matt shrugged, handed Ruska Bennie's Glock, and headed for Randi. "I don't care what you do now, Peterson. But leave me alone. I'm busy."

Randi cocked her leg for another stomp on Zambada's midsection.

"Ran, you can stop kicking Zambo."

With her hands bound behind her, and still gagged with duct tape, she ran to Matt.

He caught her shoulders and stopped her. Then gently pulled the tape from her mouth.

Randi winced.

He slipped behind her and unwrapped the tape from her wrists.

She whirled to face him.

"It's over, Ran, you—"

Her fierce hug around Matt's neck choked off his words.

He gripped her shoulders. "Are you okay? Did they hurt you?"

She blew out a blast of air. "That's all they talked about." She laid her head on his shoulder. "They were rough, and they said they would do awful things to me. But they didn't because they needed me alive."

Randi studied his eyes. "Matt, I don't know how you found me, but what you tried—you shouldn't have taken such risks."

"And you wouldn't have?"

She pulled her head back. "Matt Mathison, I would have marched into hell and back for you, if I needed to."

"That's something only one person could do, and He did it two thousand years ago. There won't be any repeats of that ... ever."

When she pulled back her head to see his face, the sun lit her hair. He smiled at the beautiful young woman with fiery hair. "Like I promised, we'll dance this night."

"Dance to 'This Night.' I got it, and it kept me going." She smiled at him through her tears.

"What did you do to this one, Matt?" Peterson boomed out. "I can't tell who he is."

Matt hooked his arm around Randi's waist, then turned and looked down at Zambada, handcuffed and lying on his side. "Zambada's a terrible receiver. He needs to learn to catch with his hands. Not his face."

Peterson glanced down at Zambada and grimaced. "He's going to need some plastic surgery if we're going to make him look like his old mug shots for the trial."

"Peterson," Ruska yelled from the Pine snag. "We need an ambulance. The EMTs will have to get this guy for us. He got stabbed by a broken tree branch. He won't give us any trouble."

"Mathison ..." Peterson stared and at him for a moment, then gave him a palms-up shrug.

"I didn't have any weapons. I had to improvise a little."

"If this is what you do when you improvise without weapons, I'm never going to give *you* a gun. Ruska, call the team and let them know we've got things under control."

Peterson pulled Zambada to his feet. "You're under—"

"Before you read him his rights, I've got something to tell him ... off the record," Matt said. "May I?" He gestured toward Zambada.

"As long as it's only words, no more rocks, go ahead." Peterson stepped aside.

Randi remained beside Peterson as Matt stood eye-to-eye with the handcuffed assassin. "Zambo, nobody intercepts my girl and runs it back all the way on me. Not you. Not Arellano. Nobody!"

Randi took his hand and pulled him away from Zambada. She circled his shoulders with her arms and clung to him. "It's over, Matt. You won. He lost."

Matt nodded and pulled her into a close embrace.

Peterson snorted. "I told Wes and Cody to chaperone these two, Ruska. Look, she's still in her pajamas."

Matt released Randi when crashing noises in the brush and trees sounded all around them.

SWAT team members moved in from all sides with lowered weapons.

"I can't believe you guys." Peterson grinned at them. "A car wreck. Unbelievable how far some people go to get out of a little work. Jim, Ron, guard our two prisoners. Lewis, call an ambulance. I need to check on the young lady who's still alone in the car, wondering what the heck happened to all of us."

"Peterson?" Randi stepped beside him. "Please call Wes and Cody. And tell them we're alright. Tell them it wasn't their fault." She closed her eyes and shook her head. "I can't imagine how they must feel."

"I'll tell them you're alright, but it's going to take a lot more than a few words for them to forgive themselves for letting Zambada get into the safe house."

"I can help them with the forgiveness part. Been there myself," Matt said.

Peterson stared at Matt until their gazes met. "Yes, I guess you have."

Randi whispered in his ear, "And I forgive you for risking your life for me ... this time. I only saw part of it, but you took out two Goliaths with your sling. Or should I say cannon?" She squeezed his right arm.

"No, Ran. No Goliaths. Just a snake and a beardless, computer-hacking Santa Claus."

Matt took Randi's hand. "Peterson, can we walk back to the car with you? Randi needs to meet the real hero here, Jennifer."

"Jennifer?" She grinned at him, her hazel eyes sparkling in the morning sun. "Should I be worried?"

"No, Ran. But Jennifer is one incredible lady. She's the one who found you."

Chapter 32

Randi walked beside Matt as they followed Agent Peterson from the chaotic scene where the SWAT team held Zambada and Bennie. The farther they walked through the trees and away from Zambada, the more her world moved toward normalcy. But there was another story that she knew nothing about. "Tell me about Jennifer, Matt."

"She's certainly beautiful." Matt gave her a smirky smile.

Randi jabbed him in the shoulder.

"Ran, Jennifer is happily married and very pregnant. She was puking her guts out this morning when Peterson called her. But she came anyway, to find you, and she did."

Randi took Matt's hand. "With morning sickness? She spent her morning figuring out how they breached the safe house and took me?"

"Unraveling the breach was the easy part. Jake and Cody did that. Jennifer did the impossible part. Rumor has it that her IQ is around two hundred, but to talk with her, you'd never know it … until she goes into action and … "

When Matt paused, she glanced at his face. Tears welled in his eyes.

"Ran, she prayed for us the entire trip over in the chopper."

If Jennifer was extremely bright, a woman of faith, maybe she could answer some of Randi's questions. It was worth a try.

Peterson sped up as they approached his car. "Let me handle Jennifer. I've gotten on the wrong side of her a few times. She has a bad temper and can get a little … intense."

The car door flew open as soon as they entered the clearing. "I heard a shot. Is everyone Okay?"

No one replied.

Jennifer jumped out of the car and faced them, hands on hips and eyes blazing. "Well, somebody better say something!"

"Yes. Everyone's safe. Mission accomplished."

She focused her intense eyes on Matt. "Peterson can't you think of some reason to lock him up? He scared me to death when he flew out the door and ran toward the—" She stopped and her eyes softened as she met Randi's gaze. "Well, I can see why Matt risked his life, but isn't somebody going to tell me what happened?"

The warm, intelligent look in Jennifer's eyes drew Randi to the small, beautiful woman. "David slew Goliath. Actually, two Goliaths with two stones."

Jennifer raised her eyebrows. "Matt, you were unarmed. You took on Zambada?"

Matt dipped his head. "Had no choice."

Randi smiled at Jennifer. "Took them both on and took them out. You should've seen Zambada's face. On the other hand, maybe it's better that you didn't."

"Peterson?" Jennifer said. "Have you got anything to add?"

"Zambada and his hacker are being loaded into ambulances. Part of our crew, the Chelan police, and some state troopers have trapped the snipers near the motel in town." He took a deep breath. "We couldn't have done this without your help, Jennifer. I'll brief your boss about today's operation, so you get the recognition you deserve. It's time to get you back to the safe house, load you on the chopper, and take you home."

Randi tugged on Peterson's sleeve. "Can I have a few minutes with her?"

He looked at Jennifer.

She nodded.

"Go ahead." He motioned toward Jennifer.

* * *

Matt's curiosity grew when Randi and Jennifer walked a short distance away and started an intense discussion. "What do you suppose they're talking about?"

Peterson raised his eyebrows. "If you don't know, it's probably about you."

"I don't think so." His gaze remained glued to the two most beautiful women he had ever seen, thankful that one of them had saved the other one and, in the process, his future.

After a few minutes, the women returned.

Randi was smiling.

Peterson gestured toward the car. "Ruska, let's get these three back to the safe house."

The chatter in the car was light, tension-reducing banter while Ruska drove them back to the other side of Lake Chelan and the mansion on the hill.

Matt held Randi's hand and listened as the two women fell into a comfortable conversation. Obviously, a deep bond was forming between them.

Peterson's cell rang as they approached the west side of Chelan. From Peterson's end of the conversation, it sounded like Wes was on the other end.

When Peterson closed his cell, he twisted in his seat toward the three in the back. "Wes said the two snipers gave themselves up. Evidently, they're not cut from the same cloth as Zambada. One of them is Arellano's baby brother. But he also gave me some intel. Arellano seems to have disappeared … dropped completely out of sight. Probably went into deep hiding."

A knot formed in his stomach. Matt didn't want to destroy the joy of the two women, but he had bad feelings about the news. "I know a little about Arellano. He's vindictive. Bent on punishing anyone who crosses him, and now you're holding his little brother, the one he planned on passing the reins to someday. He may be hiding, but I bet it's somewhere in the United States, probably in the Pacific Northwest."

He looked at the frown lines on Randi's forehead. When he thought about what Arellano would want to do to her, the knot tightened.

Chapter 33

The big sedan rolled down the lane toward the driveway of the safe house.

Safe house?

Randi wondered if she would ever again feel safe there. Would there be nightmares? Regardless, she didn't want the marshals feeling bad and moping around. They had made her and Matt's stay at the mansion a lot more endurable by their attitudes and antics.

"There they are." Peterson pointed at Wes and Cody near the door of the house, standing like soldiers at parade rest. "Two of the saddest marshals in the country, but I don't feel sorry for them."

"Well I do." Randi poked Peterson's shoulder.

He twisted toward Matt. "Is your girlfriend always so physical?"

Matt grinned at her.

She didn't return it.

"She's a touchy, feely person. Randi's not happy unless she's touching somebody."

When the car stopped in the circle drive near the door of the house, Wes pushed the front door open.

Jennifer, Randi, and Matt hurried through it while Wes and Cody shielded their bodies.

When all were safely inside, she approached Wes.

He looked down at the floor. His face held no smile and his shoulders drooped.

"We're safe, Wes."

"No thanks to us. We've never lost anyone."

"You didn't today, either."

"Like I said, no thanks to us."

"The way I heard it, you guys recognized the false video feed, told Peterson, and he brought in Jennifer." She laid her hand on his shoulder. "It took a team, Wes, and you were a part of it. I just wanted to thank you."

Wes finally met her gaze and gave her a weak smile.

"With everyone the FBI rounded up today, looks like Matt and I will be here for a while waiting for the trials to begin."

Matt hooked an arm around Randi. "And we would prefer to have you guys protecting us."

"You'll have that motley crew," Peterson said, "and a couple more marshals too. The DOJ thinks your stock is rising."

Randi had tried her best, and she would have more opportunities to convince the marshals she trusted them. But now she wanted to wash the contamination of Zambada from her body. Maybe that would help put the ordeal behind her.

"See you all in a bit. It seems that I missed my morning shower."

"First, young lady, we need to debrief, make sure we've turned over all the stones. Everybody in the kitchen in five minutes. Cody, please have someone fire up the coffee pot."

* * *

For Matt, the debriefing turned up nothing new. There had been repairs to the security system, a couple of enhancements, and its controller was disconnected from the internet. It would not be available to hackers. The marshals would only connect it briefly for system software updates. That was comforting, but the news about Arellano disappearing cancelled out that bit of comfort.

After the debriefing ended around 1:00 p.m., Matt didn't see Randi again until nearly 4:00. She spent the entire afternoon in her room doing something. Evidently something very important to her.

She had been a trooper through the entire ordeal. But a man like Zambada would've tried to terrify her into submission. He refused to dwell on the things Randi had likely heard. She had held in much about her abduction. At some point, she would need to let it out, and let it go. She was a strong woman, but Matt hoped she wasn't in her room trying to deal with the horror on her own. She needed to trust and confide in him if their relationship was going to last.

The next item on his agenda was reserving the great room for an hour this evening. He went in search of Wes and Cody. After his promise to Randi during the last Skype call, he did not want any interruptions this evening, certainly not with complaints about repeats of a certain song. Not *this night.*

For dinner, Cody brought them the spicy teriyaki take-out.

Randi sat beside him as they ate with Wes and Cody, who were soon relieved by Jake and Andy.

The mood wasn't as light and wasn't filled with the usual witty banter.

Randi was quiet. Several times during the meal she stopped eating and took his hand under the table. When they finished, she laid her head on his shoulder.

"Ran," he whispered into her ear, "I reserved the great room from 8:30 to 9:30 tonight. The marshals have been banished for the entire hour."

"When I turned and saw you throw that rock today, in one way I was surprised. In another, it was no surprise at all. After seeing you in action, Matt, I knew I could always depend on you. You're a winner, and will be at whatever you do..." She paused.

"Hey, I like this. Don't stop on my account."

"Not on your account. There's something I need to finish. But I'll meet you on the dance floor at 8:30. I promise."

She kissed his cheek, excused herself, and headed out of the dining room toward her bedroom.

Randi sounded alright. But he wondered if she really was ... and what she needed to do.

At 8:25, on his way to the great room, Matt met Cody at the foot of the stairway. "Please remind the rest of the crew the great room is off limits for the next hour."

"Only if you promise to behave. Keep the lights off and stay away from the windows." Cody's frown didn't convey anger, only worry.

"Tell the rest of the marshals we'll be careful. But I promised her this dance while Zambo had his gun to her head. If you interfere..." He grinned at Cody. "... I've got a rock just the size of your face."

"I swore I'd never do plastic surgery, no matter what. I'm outta here." Cody's smile was back. Weak, but at least it was back.

In the great room, Matt found the Billy Joel CD sitting on top of the player. He powered up the amp and the player, loaded the CD, and started the track for their song.

Movement in the entryway caught his eye. Randi walked slowly his way. Every trace of her fierce, athletic competitiveness now lay hidden.

Her green sundress contrasted with auburn curls that lay loosely on her bare shoulders. She was barefoot and that added to her feminine side, clearly on display.

Her eyes flashed the colors of the sunset still bright through the large window, bright enough to reveal the sprinkle of freckles across her nose. Her lips were full and full of color. And Randi wasn't wearing makeup. There wasn't anything that needed painting. She was perfect. She was breathtaking. And then she was in his arms.

Tonight, didn't happen accidentally like last night. This was planned. But it was still magic, magic they had chosen to experience.

Randi held him close. When the chorus swelled with the Beethoven sonata, she rested her cheek against his neck. Tears splashed onto his neck and ran down it.

He pulled her closer. "It's all over. You're safe and I intend to keep you safe forever."

"But what if something had gone wrong today and I had lost you? When I think how close I've come to losing you, I ..."

"Hush." He kissed her forehead. "The odds for us looked long about twelve hours ago, but here we are. I've got to believe God wants us together. It seems like He's been pushing us together since that moment we collided."

"Matt," she whispered through her hoarse voice, "... we didn't collide. You tackled me."

"Ran, you're a lot prettier person to tackle than a sweaty, defensive back running down the field with my interception in his grubby paws."

"I don't know quite how to reply to that."

"I do." He pulled her lips to his and kissed her, his emotions swelling with the Beethoven sonata while the voice of Billy Joel flooded the room. When their lips parted, he looked down into her tear-stained cheeks and smiling face.

"Is this song on repeat?"

"Yes. An infinite loop."

She slipped her arm around him and pressed her cheek to his chest. "Then hold me. I want to listen to the music for a while and to your heart beating. It's beating rather fast."

"Gee, I can't imagine why." He pulled his head back and scanned her hair, her face, and then focused on her eyes.

"Just hold me, Matt. Let's dance and dance until Cody comes in and shoots the stereo."

"Hey, you two. It's 9:30" Wes's voice. "Peterson just called."

Randi hooked Matt's waist with her arm.

Something important was coming. Something Wes wasn't anxious to tell them. Dread squeezed Matt's stomach into a knot.

Wes took a deep breath and blew it out slowly. "He said to tell you the federal prosecutor is flying in to talk to you two tomorrow, and that the Witness Protection Program, WITSEC, is probably on the agenda. You two will have some big decisions to make."

Chapter 34

Whenever Randi was alone with Matt, the electricity and the chemistry created feelings like nothing she had ever experienced or imagined. But as Matt turned off the stereo, and the room grew quiet, the cold, hard, real world broke the magical spell, leaving her wondering if what she had with Matt could still, somehow, be taken away from her.

Matt turned from the stereo and walked her way. His eyes widened when he saw her face, and he hurried to her, comforting her with his strong, arms. "Ran, you look worried."

"The break in, my abduction and rescue, and now the federal prosecutor's coming to talk about witness protection—it's like a snowball rolling down Mount Everest."

"Know what you mean. I didn't think they would force the issue so quickly."

"It frightens me. More life changes. But they can't steal what you and I—"

"No. They can't. As long as we are committed to each other, there will be a way for us. The DOJ won't force us apart."

"Why tomorrow, Matt?"

"Put yourself in the prosecutor's place. You've got two witnesses who you need if you're going to put away the bad guys. You have enough of the cartel in custody to severely damage the organization. What's your biggest worry?"

"That the witnesses won't testify?"

"That's right. If we can be intimidated by the cartel, or if we fear the DOJ is going to use us then leave us as targets in a shooting gallery—"

"Okay. I get your point. They're coming to reassure us, get a commitment from us to testify, and use the witness protection program to accomplish that. But I've heard that only families go into that program together. Is that really true?"

He pulled her gently to the couch and sat beside her. "The program is pretty much kept under wraps. But that's what I've heard too. So, what are we going to do about that?"

They were on the threshold of making lifetime commitments to each other. It was what she believed she wanted, but it was coming so fast.

When she looked into his warm, caring eyes, her worries melted away ... all but one.

"Ran, whatever is bothering you, I'd like to help."

"I'm not sure you *can* help. This doesn't concern you."

"If it concerns you, it concerns me." Matt raised his eyebrows. "It's your parents, isn't it?"

"Yeah." She pulled her head back to see his face. "By going into WITSEC, I feel that I'm throwing them to the wolves ... or the demons."

"You're taking too much on your shoulders. That's God's domain." He pulled her head against his neck. "Interesting problem though. So what advice did Miss Universe, the woman with the two hundred IQ, give you? That is what you talked about isn't it?"

"Yeah. I've never felt confident enough to stand up to my atheistic parents like a believer should. You know, always be prepared to give an answer to anyone for our hope. My parents are experts in their fields, physics and biology."

"And you thought somebody like Einstein, somebody who was a believer, could give you that confidence?"

She nodded. "Besides that, you can tell in an instant Jennifer's somebody you can trust."

"You've got that right. I was about to lose my mind until she stepped into the room this morning and convinced me she could find you. Well, what did she tell you?"

"She had a lot of ideas, but basically, she said it was time for me to stop licking my wounds and to let them heal. She told me to write my parents a letter. Tell them I love and forgive them and why I chose Christianity—a short, pithy version, one they, as scientists, can understand, but one they can't easily refute."

"What a homework assignment. And you probably want to win the Nobel Peace Prize with this letter."

"There's more. Two years ago, Jennifer was an agnostic. But Jennifer's husband is something of a Christian apologist, so she gave me some good ideas to point the way for people like Mom and Dad." She peered deeply into his blue eyes. "You're a writer. Would you read my letter before I send it?"

"I'm certainly no apologist. But sure. What's it worth to you?"

"A kiss."

"That's all?"

"What do you mean, that's all? Maybe you don't mean it when you—"

Ran, I mean it when I kiss you. But I had something else in mind. Something like I get to ask you a question, and you promise to answer in the affirmative."

"A blank check? I never give anyone—" She stopped. She trusted Matt to care for her feelings, protect them, to protect her. In her heart she knew it was safe to answer yes to any serious question this man asked her, especially the one that was coming.

* * *

Matt gathered his courage and tried to will the drum in his chest to slow from allegro to andante.

"Miranda Richards, will—"

"Matt, I told you how I feel about that name."

"You told me a lot of things that day. And I told you—" He was getting sidetracked and this wasn't a time to bring up anything unpleasant. "May I start again?"

"Yeah. Please do."

"Randi Richards..."

"Yes, I'll marry you."

"Nothing like keeping a guy in suspense."

"Oh ... it's suspense you want. Okay. I'll marry you, but it's on one condition."

Matt's voice caught in his throat. Randi Richards had promised to marry him. Well, on one condition. Now she wore her enigmatic smile. For a man who had bottomed out, sojourned in the far country, landed in a pit of miry clay, one who was a recent fugitive from a drug cartel's assassin, it was unbelievable. "Okay. Let me hear your escape clause."

"Matt, how could you possibly think—"

"I'm not sure I can think at all right now. Maybe I should call for Wes or Cody."

She pulled her head back. "If you do, I'll kill you. We're not finished."

"Not finished?"

"Two conditions."

"Two? Are you backing out?"

"Nope."

He needed to close this deal before it, somehow, slipped away to three, four or more. "What are the two conditions?"

"First, you have to critique my letter to my parents, and second, you must court me—a good, old-fashioned courtship—until we have to give the DOJ our answer about WITSEC."

"That's an offer I can't refuse. But, with the attorney coming in the morning, ours could be the shortest courtship on record."

"Yeah. Or, depending on what this lawyer says, one with a big question mark stamped on it."

Chapter 35

When the U. S. attorney walked into the dining room, Randi involuntarily stood.

Dressed in a navy business suit, with short, dark hair and intelligent, penetrating, dark eyes, Ms. Jessica Holt, the prosecutor, looked the part of someone who could destroy a lame response or a weak alibi like tissue paper in a cross-cut paper shredder running a two-horsepower motor.

Matt seemed to have the same response to this thirty-something woman who commanded respect.

Ms. Holt stepped to their side of the dining room table and offered her hand to Matt. "I'm Jessica Holt. Hello, Matt." She turned to Randi. "Hello, Randi." Her hands were calloused, rough, and her grip was strong. What did this woman do in her spare time? Swing a splitting mall?

"Please sit down. We need to cover a lot in a short time. Things are a little busy in Western District Court in Washington State, thanks in a large part to you two." She studied their faces for a moment, then opened a folder. "We have impaneled a special grand jury to indict these cartel members. To get that indictment, we need your testimony."

Randi opened her mouth to speak.

Ms. Holt shoved a palm at Randi. "Please hold your questions for a moment. If you testify, we are certain the jury will bring indictments against the defendants on several charges." She studied their faces. "But once you testify, you will be more visible to those who want to retaliate, so we want you to know that, if you testify, I am authorized by the Department of Justice to offer you protection in WITSEC, the U.S. Federal Witness Protection Program."

Randi couldn't hold her questions inside. Life was changing again, and she needed to know what the changes meant. There wasn't another runner to stare down. Ice woman had melted.

Please, Lord, keep me calm and sane.

Ms. Holt looked from Matt to Randi. "We'll brief you more completely on the program when you come to Seattle to testify before the grand jury."

"When will that be?"

"Day after tomorrow."

A day and a half? "May we ask you a few more questions now?"

Jessica Holt glanced at a legal pad, then met Randi's gaze. "I need to go over the questions I'm going to ask you in front of the grand jury. That will take at least an hour. Then I have to rush back to Seattle. We'll answer all of your questions in a couple of days."

Matt laid his hand over hers. "Randi obviously has some questions and so do I. Isn't there anything you can tell us today?"

A flicker of a smile tweaked the corners of the prosecutor's mouth. "Okay. A question apiece."

Matt nudged her shoulder. "Go ahead, Ran."

She gave Matt a nervous smile then turned her attention to Ms. Holt. "Will I get a chance to say goodbye to my parents?"

"Possibly, but only if they are willing to follow our schedule and a strict set of guidelines."

Randi knew they may not agree to see her at all, let alone inconvenience themselves to do so. Her proximity to organized crime may further alienate them. She couldn't count on bidding them farewell. She could almost count on that *not* happening. Her letter, the one Jennifer suggested, was taking on more significance.

Matt glanced from Randi to the prosecutor. "What about Randi and me?"

"Your situation is a bit unusual. I've never dealt with unmarried people who ..." She hesitated. Her gaze moved back and forth between them.

"Who love each other." Matt finished for her.

Randi took his hand. "What if that situation changed to legally married?"

Ms. Holt cleared her throat. "We would need be certain about your marital status in advance of our preparation to place you in the program."

Randi squeezed Matt's hand. "And when would the preparation to place us start?"

"A few days from the time we knew you were accepting our offer to enter WITSEC."

Didn't she understand? Randi needed to nail down dates, times, and decisions. "How long might that be from now?"

Ms. Holt pursed her lips and shook her head. "I can't say for sure."

"Give us an educated guess?"

"Maybe two weeks."

The snowball down Mount Everest had picked up speed. "Two weeks? So ... you need an answer in two days and verification of our legal status in two weeks?"

More tight lips came from Ms. Holt. "That sounds about right."

Randi gripped Matt's hand fearing she might lose her sanity. "That sounds so rushed. So..."

"Look." Ms. Holt closed the manila folder. "WITSEC is a radical life change. When doctors enter this program, they can't practice medicine any more. Teachers can't teach. It's a completely new identity. On paper, you bring nothing from your past with you. If two single people enter, it would be overly complicated, perhaps dangerous, to place them in the same city, especially in a small town. Think about it—"

"I already have." Randi looked at Matt.

He met her gaze but said nothing.

"Does that mean you'll both give me your answer after we meet in two days at the Federal Courthouse in Seattle?"

Randi nodded.

Matt squeezed her hand. "We will."

Ms. Jessica Holt pulled out a notepad with a long, hand-written list on it, the prosecutor's questions. "Okay, Matt and Randi. Time for the dress rehearsal."

* * *

A restless night left Matt fuzzy headed. Too many thoughts about the impending trial, the Witness Protection Program, and his unfinished romantic thriller. Not the manuscript, the real life romantic thriller, the one he would give anything to be able to mold and fashion as he did the characters and stories in his novel.

He rolled out of bed and slipped into a T-shirt, shorts, and his running shoes. Through the covered window, the brightness of the sun said this was another typical summer day in Chelan. The temperature would be in the nineties. But in his five-thousand-square-foot prison, once again it would be seventy-two degrees. His running shoes would not be loping on a sandy beach with Randi. They would be jogging on a treadmill.

He trudged down the hallway toward the kitchen, feeling like the huddle had broken without him calling a play. Now he walked into the kitchen, the line of scrimmage.

Randi stood at the counter, pouring herself a cup of coffee.

"How did you sleep last night, Ran?"

"Sleep? What's that?" She turned her head and shot him a glance over the auburn curls resting on her shoulders.

He smiled. "Me too."

She turned to face him, coffee cup in hand. "What's the formula for romance? In your writing, I mean."

"The main thing is that the story ends with the hero and the heroine together, both happy."

Randi sat down at the table and set her cup in front of her.

He took a seat across the table from her. "Tomorrow they fly us to Seattle to testify. Are you nervous?"

Randi took a sip of her coffee and met his gaze. "Yes, I'm nervous. I've never been in a court room, let alone been on the witness stand. And I've certainly never testified while a man who wants to kill me is staring at me like he's ready to do it."

"He won't be there for the indictment part. And he can't hurt you, Ran. So don't worry."

She studied him and, from the look in her eyes, she knew exactly what he was thinking. Randi could do that. It was another reason, among the hundreds he was accumulating, that they needed be together.

"Matt, you've turned your life around completely, and by testifying you're helping to dismantle this cartel."

"The federal prosecutor will agree with you." He shook his head. "But when this goes to trial, that's not the picture the defense attorney will paint. And I won't know how he'll attack me until I'm on the stand." He reached across the table and took her hand.

She looked down at their clasped hands, her lips parted but silent.

"Whatever you hear, I'm not the man I was. I never will be again." He looked down at the floor.

"I'm good at separating truth from fiction. Especially when I know a person's character."

She was staring at him, but he couldn't look up.

"Please, Matt, look at me."

He looked at their intertwined hands.

"No. At my eyes."

He met her gaze fully. The light from the skylight above lit the mixture of red colors in her hair and the greens in her hazel eyes.

"Tell me what you see."

Everything that comprised Randi Richards, her warmth, the fire of her hair and the fire of her fierce competitor's heart, her love, her passion ... she was offering it all to him.

Randi stood. "I need you, Matt, every bit as much as I did when you saved my life. Save my life again. Please. Marry me, before it's too late."

He stood and turned toward her. "Wasn't that supposed to be my line?"

"If it's your line, don't you think you'd better say it?"

He pulled Randi close, much closer than he ever had.

* * *

Randi relaxed in Matt's arms and waited for the quarterback to call the play.

"Ran, you can trust me."

"I do trust you. Completely."

"But my past isn't—"

"Isn't important anymore. It's in the past. Gone. As far as the east is from the west. Gone and forgotten."

He gave her his confident, winning smile. "Then, Randi, will you marry me ... now?"

She returned his smile. "I hope I'm not going to have to initiate everything in this marriage."

This man had quarterbacked football teams, led them in the heat of battle. Randi was sure that God hadn't created Matt to be a timid man. He was meant to lead and, whenever he had taken the lead, incredible things happened. Lives were saved. Criminals were captured. Her heart was stolen, stolen and carried away into captivity, far beyond any possibility of rescue.

"Ran ... your answer?"

She displayed her coy smile for him. "You did promise to meet all of my conditions, so I guess I'm obligated to answer in the affirmative."

"I release you from all obligations. Now, answer my question."

"How long do you suppose it will take to get a marriage license, given that we can't leave the safe house? Do you think Jennifer would be willing to be my matron of honor? I hope she doesn't puke during the ceremony. Who's going to stand with you, Matt?"

Matt's face beamed. "I'll take that as a yes."

Chapter 36

"Ran, come on. Peterson's waiting and—" Matt's voice, mind, and nearly his heart stopped, when Randi stepped from her room and into the hallway.

He had seen her in a simple summer dress at church, but never dressed like this. Randi wore a navy-blue blazer and a matching skirt that looked custom-tailored for her tall, perfectly shaped body.

Her waves of auburn hair, ending in loose curls on her shoulders, were animated by Randi's graceful walk, a natural walk that would be the envy of any fashion model.

Matt found himself gawking at her like a teenage kid would at a Hollywood idol. He took her hand and led Randi to the front door of the house.

The whine of the chopper's engine started.

Matt slipped out of his suit coat. "It's too hot for coats out there." He helped Randi out of her jacket. "Are you ready for today?"

"Yes. But it appears that you aren't." She gave him a corner-of-the-eye glance. "I've seen enough of your gaga eyes, Mr. Mathison. And I'm not flattered ... well, not much."

She smiled, sending his mind into another delirium.

Peterson appeared in the doorway. "The marshals are ready. We're clear outside, so let's load up."

Wes stepped beside them on their left, carrying an automatic.

Cody took the front.

Peterson took their right and prodded Cody. "Hurry up. Let's get them airborne where it's safe."

They double-timed to the chopper.

Randi and Matt slid in the back.

Wes took the right side, laying his assault rifle in his lap.

Peterson slid in beside the pilot and looked up the hill for an all clear from Andy.

The young marshal waved the all-clear sign, and the engine revved.

The rotor spun up until the chopper lifted slowly off the pad.

Matt looked down at the large house that had become both a home and a prison. A movement near the ridge top caught his attention.

Cody waved frantically at them, then he pointed up the hill. No one else seemed to notice Cody.

Matt opened his mouth to speak, but his voice caught in his throat when he followed Cody's gesture up the hill.

Some kind of aircraft, flying very low, had topped the hill and now it accelerated down the slope, heading directly for the slowly rising helicopter.

Matt tried again to speak but choked on his words. Finally, they exploded from his mouth. "An aircraft coming in at five o'clock!"

Peterson's head spun around.

The small plane looked like a drone. It bore down on them rapidly, about four hundred yards away.

"Outrun it!" Peterson yelled at Mac.

"No time!" Mac shouted back.

Matt had been trained to look downfield, to see everything and react. His training took over. "Spin the chopper! Wes, you've gotta take it out!"

Mac tugged on the controls and the aircraft spun around, placing Wes on the side nearest the approaching airplane. "Shove the door open, Wes!"

"Will the rotor suck it up?"

"Just do it!" Mac yelled.

Wes released his belt, swiveled toward the door, and shoved it open with his feet.

The drone raced to within two hundred yards.

Wes raised his assault rifle.

The drone closed to one hundred fifty yards.

He fired a burst.

No explosion. Nothing.

The airplane zoomed down on them, now less than one hundred yards away.

Matt's seatbelt was already off. He wrapped his body around Randi's.

Fifty yards out. It headed straight for the helicopter's rotor.

Wes fired again.

The drone exploded.

The shock wave slammed into the chopper.

Fragments of the airplane blew holes in the window near Matt's shoulder.

Other shrapnel smacked into the rotor.

The helicopter yawed and spun in response.

Mac's hands jerked on the controls.

Matt pinned Randi's body against the seat with his. "I love you, Ran."

She wrapped her arms around him.

Mac's movements slowed.

The helicopter stopped spinning and fell with the rotating blades reducing the fall rate.

He dropped the chopper onto the landing pad.

Matt and Randi slammed down into the seat.

The open door broke off and clattered across the concrete pad.

When they were solidly down on the pad, Matt slid off from Randi and scanned her for blood. He released the breath he'd been holding when he saw none.

She stared into his eyes, wide-eyed. "Matt ..."

Cody's face appeared in front of Wes's door.

"How many roads lead out of here?" Peterson yelled at Cody as the rotor spun down.

"Two. Andy's on the phone. State troopers and the Chelan Police should be dispatched in a few more seconds. They won't get away," Cody said.

Matt grabbed Peterson's shoulder. "Arellano's in the area. The homemade drone has his signature all over it."

"Then he made a big mistake." Peterson's brow furled into deep frown lines.

"I told you he's vindictive."

"Is anybody hit?" Peterson asked.

"Matt's hit!" Randi cried out.

"No, I'm not."

"Matt, your head." Her face contorted as she looked at him.

"You're a bloody mess." Wes studied his head.

"And you sound like a Brit." Matt ran his fingers through his hair. They came away dripping blood. "Doesn't hurt. Must be a scalp wound."

Wes grabbed his arm and pulled him toward the opened door of the helicopter. "Let's get you into the house and check you out."

Cody, Wes, and Peterson escorted Matt and Randi to the house while Mac inspected his helicopter.

From several directions, distant sirens screamed.

In the kitchen, Wes washed the blood from Matt's scalp while Peterson watched in silence.

Randi held his hand.

Inside Matt a slow burning fuse had been lit.

Wes breathed a slow sigh. "You were right, Matt. Only a deep scratch. But that was way too close for comfort."

"Doesn't matter." Matt said it didn't, but anger grew inside him as he contemplated the incident. "Arellano failed. And this attempt might get him caught. But, Peterson, what would have happened if that radio-controlled plane had hit us?"

Peterson shook his head. "The way it exploded, there was likely a pound of C-4 onboard. It would have blown up the chopper and killed us all. It was a clever attack. They must have launched it from the ridge."

"I've been over that ridge several times," Cody said. "There's a field on the other side where the locals fly their radio-controlled model planes. No one would have noticed anything until the explosion. But they would have had to control it from the top of the ridge."

Peterson glanced from Cody to Matt. "Then Cody's right. If they were on the ridge, they won't get away."

"It was Arellano." Matt's voice turned to a growl. "Get us to Seattle, Peterson! There's only one way to stop these people."

He felt Randi's gaze on him. He had felt it since they entered the house. But he didn't return it. Matt didn't want her to see the depth of his anger toward the people who had nearly taken her life.

She released his hand and cupped his cheeks, pulling his face toward her. "Look at me, Matt. I'm not going to risk losing you."

"There is only one way to stop them. We testify, starting today, and we lock them up for life."

"I know you're right. But you don't have a clue how badly you scared me when you shielded me. And then I saw the blood." Her voice broke.

With Randi holding his face, Matt couldn't avoid her eyes. Her pain and fear doused his flaming anger. He pulled her close. "It's my fault that you're in danger. There's no way I'll let them hurt you."

"After all you've done, you don't have anything to prove to me. And the way you took charge with that flying bomb bearing down on us. Matt, I trust you completely and I need you. So please don't take any more chances."

When he looked up to ask Peterson about the helicopter, he saw that everyone had left the kitchen, letting them have their discussion in private.

"Peterson?" Matt called out.

The tall man's profile filled the doorway. "You've got about forty-five minutes until another chopper arrives."

"Will we make it in time?"

"Ruska just called me and said the judge is going to call for a one-hour recess due to our ... uh, problems. You will get to testify today, and with a little luck, we'll have some bigger fish to fry the next time the grand jury meets."

"Thanks. Please excuse us now. Randi and I have another issue to sort out."

"Remember, you've only got forty-five minutes."

"Matt, we don't have any other issues to—"

He held her shoulders and watched her hazel eyes glitter. Smelled the scent of her hair. To miss out on life with Randi—he wouldn't let that happen.

"Matt," Randi's voice was soft, hardly more than a whisper. "Let's ask them if they'll take us to city hall when we get back. This is Monday. We could marry as soon as Thursday. After four close calls, I don't want to miss ... us."

"I need to call Jennifer and ask Peterson if it's possible for her to come."

"I'm going to ask Wes to stand with me."

Randi frowned. "Who should we get to marry us?"

"I wonder if there's any way Pastor Santos from Forks could—"

"I know." Randi's eyes widened. "Everyone says Peterson likes Jennifer, almost like a daughter. If she asked to come, and if Pastor Santos could come to Seattle, maybe Peterson would let them both fly here on Thursday."

"Helicopter flights aren't cheap, but Peterson already has a reason to fly here Thursday." But Matt shouldn't be the one to ask him. He had violated Peterson's direct orders too many times. "*You'd* better ask him, Ran. I'm not sure he likes me much, especially after I've interfered with his plans and disobeyed him during some pretty intense situations."

"C'mon, Matt. I've seen how he looks at you. Sure, he got mad, but he respects you. Peterson knows a good man when he sees one." Randi cupped his cheek. "You *are* a good man."

"And you're a good woman. That and a whole lot more. But I've got an important question to ask you."

"We've already asked all the important questions."

"No, there's one more. Do you snore, Ran? Because, if you do—"

Randi's arm swung and a loaf of bread from the counter thumped hard on Matt's head, sending slices of bread sliding across the kitchen floor.

"You two need to quit loafing around." Peterson's voice boomed into the room. "The chopper's here. Time to tell that grand jury what these guys are really like. We just caught two more cartel members. One of them is wounded. When you get back, we need to swing by the jail and see if you can identify them."

Randi caught Peterson's gaze. "Can we stop by city hall on the way to the jail?"

Peterson smiled. "That can probably be arranged."

Chapter 37

In Seattle, Jessica Holt had presented an airtight, condemning case to the grand jury.

Matt and Randi's return trip from Seattle had been uneventful.

After the chopper landed in Chelan, the marshals escorted them to a car with Jake at the wheel.

Andy rode shotgun with something a bit more powerful than a shotgun in his lap.

Matt slid in beside Randi and studied her pensive expression. "Don't worry, Ran. The indictment is in the bag."

"I know. But I fumbled for words so many times that—"

"But you didn't fumble the ball. You did fine. Now let's see if we can get this marriage license pushed through. Bureaucracies of any size worry me."

"You're pretty good at getting things done when you set your mind to it. You'll think of something."

"I guess I have to after Peterson agreed to bring the chopper on Thursday. I missed the last part of that conversation. How did you ever get him to agree to bring both Jennifer and Pastor Santos?

"I said that Jennifer would never forgive him if he didn't, and that neither would you."

"Me? Matt, the dealer, doesn't have much clout with the FBI."

"Like I told you before, Peterson respects you. You're his kind of guy."

"If you're right, maybe we can ask Peterson to grease the skids with the city of Chelan and have them push our marriage license through the local paper mill."

"I know he wouldn't refuse, but I haven't heard what Wes said about being your best man."

"I cornered him in the men's room at the courthouse. I had him at a disadvantage ... and he agreed. He stands beside me at 3:00 p.m. on Thursday and then he's rid of us. Well ... the stage is set for getting rid of us once the trials are over." He paused. "By the way, what were you and Jennifer talking about today? The way you were hiding, it must have been top secret."

"No comment."

Probably about a wedding dress. Randi's sundress would have suited him, but she probably wanted a white dress, and she deserved one.

Andy's cell played the WSU fight song, not music to Matt's Husky ears. "It's Peterson. Let's see if he has any news from district court." Andy answered the call. "Agent Taylor here. ... Yes. ... All four of them? ... Good. Yes, we're taking good care of them." Andy turned toward the back seat with a grin spanning the width of his face.

"We're going to trial, right?" Matt asked.

"Yep," Andy replied. "All four indicted on all counts, and the grand jury will hear evidence against the other guys next week. Let's go down to the jail and see what size fish the local police caught."

Randi squeezed his hand. "See, everything is turning out as it should." The pensive look on her face returned and then morphed into a warm smile. "If anyone had told me a few months ago that I'd be getting married in Chelan, Washington in June, I would have called them a lunatic. Things can change in a hurry when you bump into the right person."

"But, Ran, it helps when the right Person orchestrates the bump."

After they arrived at the Chelan jail, Andy introduced Matt and Randi to the police chief, who led them to a room in the jail with a large, flat-screen video monitor which showed the interior of an empty room. Soon three armed guards escorted two men into the room.

Matt studied the short, muscular Hispanic, with a light complexion, who limped into the room. "Chief, the wounded guy is Arellano. The taller guy, I think I've seen before, but I don't know who he is."

"I'm afraid I can't help you out with these two." Randi shrugged. "But I'm glad you caught them."

"I'm pretty sure the tall guy is the explosives expert," the Chief said. "Forensics will nail him if that's the case. He'll be covered with evidence."

After they left the jail, Matt engaged the Chief in a conversation about the arrests and the grand jury trial. When the chief told him that the arrest of the Tijuana Cartel's boss, Arellano, was likely the most notable achievement in the department's history, Matt hit him with his request to expedite the processing of the marriage license. The strategy worked.

* * *

On this, the eve of their wedding, Randi's parents still had not responded to phone messages from the U. S. Marshals. Matt knew about the pain of rejection, but Randi hadn't deserved it. He had.

Peterson had graciously agreed to stand in and give away the bride.

Somehow Matt and Randi had made all the necessary legal and other desired arrangements for their wedding. But Randi had demanded that he meet her at 7:00 pm in the great room. At 6:59 Matt closed the door to his room, a room that would be his for only one more night. Tomorrow evening they would leave on their honeymoon, a trip of thirty feet down the hallway to Randi's bedroom suite, their home for the next several months.

When Matt entered the great room another Billy Joel classic played softly on the stereo, *Just the Way You Are.* Was dancing on the agenda for tonight? He hoped so.

Randi sat on the sofa with a notebook in her lap. She wore maroon and white Texas A&M shorts and a white T-shirt. It looked like the running clothes she wore the day they met on the trail.

"Come here, Matt." She reached for his hand and pulled him onto the sofa beside her. "Look. No mud."

"I thought that outfit looked familiar. Just for your info, I checked you out again anyway."

"So I noticed. Look while you can, because you won't see me again until tomorrow afternoon."

"Yes. But after that, Ran ..."

Her face turned a brighter shade of red than her hair. "Changing the subject, I—"

"Why change the subject?"

"Because I need your help."

"With what's in the notebook?"

"Yeah. I need you to critique my letter to my parents. I want your opinion."

"About opinions. Everybody's got one, so they aren't worth much in the market place of ideas."

"But yours is worth a lot to me. Matt, I don't want to be preachy, but they need to know there are valid reasons for my beliefs, more valid than the reasons for their own. They also need to know that I love and forgive them. Read it and tell me what you think."

The contents of the notebook were so important to the woman he loved, his hand shook as he took it from her. "So at last I get to see some of *your* writing."

"But this isn't fiction."

"That's too bad. You know, authors get to play God. If this were fiction, we could make things turn out right." Matt settled into the couch with the notebook and began reading.

Randi draped an arm around his shoulders and leaned close, following along as his eyes scanned each line.

Dear Mom and Dad,

Please read this letter. I may never get an opportunity to send another. So I want to tell you I love you both very much, and I forgive you for your part in our disagreements. Please forgive me for mine.

I am in the process of testifying against some very evil people, people who never forgive and never forget. I will soon be given a new identity, but don't worry about me. God has blessed me with a wonderful man, a strong and loving protector, who will become my husband tomorrow, and he will enter this new life with me.

Since this may be my last communication with you, I'm trying to leave nothing unsaid. Please understand.

You both put a lot of stock in science to guide you to the truth. But please consider that science and the scientific method are founded on a set of metaphysical presuppositions which, if not true, neither is science. If you think about it, that makes all truth fundamentally metaphysical in nature, just like my faith in God.

I can clearly remember that day when I walked into my first Meteorology 101 class at Texas A&M. The professor wrote out the equation of motion for air. This differential equation filled three large whiteboards, extending halfway around the room. But even that equation was only a feeble attempt to model the complexity of the earth's atmosphere. No computer could possibly solve that equation. After the professor made thirty or forty simplifying assumptions, he obtained a crude model computable by the world's most powerful computers.

When a person studies Meteorology, the gap between man's finite knowledge and our creator God's infinite knowledge is readily apparent. Mom and Dad, I'm guessing that you've seen the same thing in biology and physics. Since we cannot know everything, God's existence, outside the realm of our knowledge, is completely plausible. I believe His existence is necessary, otherwise there would be nothing.

If possible, I will try to send an occasional letter to you through a U.S. marshal, but letters will only be delivered if they deem it to be safe. Perhaps you could start a blog that tells me what is happening with you. I could read it. But if you do, please make no reference to me.

Goodbye, Mom. Goodbye, Dad. I love you. You are in my thoughts and prayers.

Matt closed the notebook. "Wow. You gave them things to think on without preaching. And you didn't give them much wiggle room. Good points, clear and concise. Honestly, Ran, I wouldn't change a word."

She squeezed him and kissed his cheek. "Thanks. But I can't take credit for all of it. Jennifer helped me. Now, come on. We have enough time to dance to our song, then I have to leave. We wouldn't want to give ourselves bad luck."

"Ran, it's not Thursday for four and a half more hours."

"The song is on repeat. C'mon. Let's drive Cody crazy."

"Like you're doing to me?" Matt pulled her into his arms. "We can save that for tomorrow too."

* * *

Randi walked down the hallway behind Jennifer. With a flower in her hair, Jennifer looked like a Hawaiian princess as she continued to the arched entryway to the great room while *Aloha Oe* played on the stereo.

Randi peeked around the entryway to the great room and waived to Cody.

His hand moved to the stereo controls. Soon a ukulele began playing softly. After a few measures, the expression-filled voice of a woman sang the words to the Hawaiian Wedding Song, and Randi stepped into the room.

Clearly audible above the music, Matt sucked in a breath of air when he saw her in her wedding dress. His smile was new to her. It conveyed more than his words ever had.

Tears filled her eyes when she saw Matt brushing his own tears away.

A panorama of her last two years played through Randi's mind as she walked slowly to meet Matt. God had blessed her with a relationship with Himself, giving her more than she'd ever imagined she would have. Then much of it was snatched away by her parent's rejection. Matt entered the drama, bringing danger, then protection, devotion, and finally an overwhelming love that moved her in strange, new, wonderful ways she couldn't have imagined a few months ago.

Matt took her hands and Pastor Santos guided them through vows that bound them inextricably in a relationship that would last a lifetime.

Too soon the ceremony was over. She had become Mrs. Randi Mathison ... until WITSEC gave them their new names. The names didn't matter. All that mattered was she was Matt's and he was hers. Completely.

Pastor Santos nodded to Matt. "You may kiss your bride."

Matt stepped close, wrapping her in his strong, comforting arms. Slowly he closed the distance between their faces.

Randi was there waiting when their lips met.

Epilogue

6 Months later, somewhere in the U. S.

From his large easy chair, Matt glanced over the top of the morning newspaper at his wife.

She sat at their desk in the family room, squirming in front of her laptop. She was beautiful, but obviously not comfortable.

"The deposit cleared. How does it feel to be a millionaire, Ran?"

Something quickly damped out Randi's growing smile. "We could have been that five times over if you weren't so generous. But I'm glad you gave it away. Maybe it will keep some ministries going through this tough economy ... and keep some kids away from drugs."

He lowered the newspaper into his lap. "That was the plan. But putting Arellano away permanently was worth a whole lot more than five million dollars."

"Matt, put down the paper and come here."

"First, listen to this. Arellano started serving his life sentence in the federal prison yesterday ... along with his goons who preceded him."

"That's what they paid us for. Although I didn't really expect we would get that reward money. But, Matt?"

"I'm coming."

Randi grabbed her midsection with one hand. With the other she snatched the trash can by the desk. "Oh, crud!"

She lost her breakfast.

He jumped up and ran to her side. "Are you okay?"

"No. But I will be as soon as—" She retched again.

"You're sick, Ran."

"No lie."

This sounded familiar, somehow. "Are you pregnant?"

"I was waiting for a good time to break the news. The doctor said yes, but she also—"

"That's great."

"That's easy for you to say ..."

"I love you so much." He put his arms around her.

"Don't squeeze me, Matt. You might get more than you bargained for." She took a slow, easy breath.

He relaxed his arms. "So what else did the doctor say?"

"That I need to see her again in *two* weeks ... *two* being the operative word."

Twins. Was she serious? "You wouldn't joke about something like that, would you?"

"It's only a suspicion at this point. That's why I planned to keep it a secret for a few days. But the cat's out of the bag now."

He reached for the odious trash can. "It's hardly a cat. And I think it's time to take the bag out of the house."

"Not yet. I might need it again. But I'll definitely be shortening my runs and doing them in the evenings ... *not* the mornings."

His news wasn't as momentous, nor would it be as welcome as hers. "Uh ... I've got some news too." He bit his lip and flashed her a glance.

"What have you done now, Matt Moore?" She pushed her face within a foot of his, staring into his eyes.

"You know something? You've got really bad breath."

"Gee, I wonder why? It's all your fault, you know." She moved back a step. "But what were you about to tell me?"

He blasted out a sigh and prepared for a backlash. "The high school football coach has these two promising quarterbacks on his team, but he needs an assistant, a quarterback coach who can develop them." He pursed his lips and studied her face. "So ... what do you think? Is it too—"

"Do it." She took his hand. "It's who you are, who you need to be. But, Matt ..." She squeezed his hand and pled with her eyes. "Please don't take them to the state championship. The publicity would—"

"Twins. A coaching position. You really made my day."

"The day is only beginning. The reason I called you over here is to show you what Mom wrote on her blog last night. Listen to this." She read slowly, her voice quivering.

A few months ago, I said dogmatically that there was no God. But if God is an infinite being, as many claim, then I was claiming to be infinite myself. Well, at a minimum, I was claiming outright omniscience. Otherwise, God might exist somewhere outside the scope of my knowledge. As someone pointed out to me, this is a metaphysical issue, one that transcends science, which is itself built on metaphysical presuppositions.

As a scientist, my discovery left me no choice but to investigate this sort of being, the omniscient, and possibly omnipotent, God. Does this being exist? If so, does He have personhood? Is He good? And how does one perform such an investigation? What evidence do you evaluate?

Randi's voice caught once, then choked again. She couldn't continue.

"I'll finish sweetheart." He found where she had left off.

My husband and I have recently begun attending something called Alpha. It's a loosely structured series of meetings where all questions are allowed, especially questions about the existence and nature of God. We've both come to appreciate and to love the people who have pointed us in the right direction, those conducting Alpha as well as other people in our lives. We thank them all so much for caring about us.

They had sent Randi a clear message. "Ran, she's practically regurgitating the words in your letter."

Randi clutched her midsection. "No more talk about regurgitating. Please?"

"Sorry." He put his hand over hers on her capricious stomach. "But you hardly have to read between the lines.

She's saying that they *love* you, *appreciate* you, and *know* that you care about them."

Tears poured from Randi's flooded eyes, splashing on his shirt. "I know. I *finally* know." She swiped her cheeks. "I love them so much, Matt. But will I ever be able to see them and tell them face to face?"

"If the cartel dies, maybe someday we can quietly slip out of hiding, at least enough for our parents to come and visit us. He's a big God. He can make it safe enough for us to do that. He's also—what did C. S. Lewis call Him—the Hound of Heaven?"

Randi nodded. "Yeah. That's what he called Him. But that's from a poem by Francis Thompson. And despite everything that happened, He always kept us safe." She laid her head on his shoulder. "I think we've found the best place on earth for us. Being together and in the center of His will—that's the only safe place."

He kissed her forehead and smiled. "But for your parents, with the Hound of Heaven on their trail, there *is* no safe place."

The End

Author's Notes

No Safe Place was my NaNoWriMo novel for 2013. As such, I wrote it in the first twenty-seven days of November. A few things have changed in the setting since I wrote this story. I've left them in, keeping them contemporary to 2013 in order to avoid major changes to the plot. However, residents of Forks, or people who frequently visit the area, will realize that cell phone coverage is now continuous from Highway 101, along La Push Road and Mora Road, to the beaches. If I remember correctly, in 2015 cell coverage made it to Rialto Beach, across the river from La Push. But to keep my protagonists from calling for help when they were being chased by the cartel's assassin, I left the cell coverage as it was in 2013.

On the trail to 2nd Beach, the steps down to the beach were dug into the steep hillside. Consequently, they vary greatly in length. I made them more uniform in my story, so Matt and Randi could run down them. Please don't try to run down them as my characters did. They took a tumble, but you'll probably end up in the Forks Hospital emergency room.

Regarding Randi's job, sending up the radiosonde from the old Quillayute air strip—at the time I wrote *No Safe Place*, the weather services at Quillayute had been contracted out to a small firm in Port Angeles. The people who launched the radiosonde had to make the hour-long drive to UIL (the airport designator for Quillayute) once or twice a day, depending on whether they stayed all day. Currently, the weather services at Quillayute have been contracted with The Rockhill Group (TRG) which supplies weather services for several locations in the U.S., including weather observations for NOAA National Weather Services at the old Quillayute airstrip.

Lake Chelan is as beautiful as I described in the story, probably more so. I became intimately acquainted with the area thirty-eight years ago, when my wife and I and our three kids boxed up enough supplies to last us for a week and headed for Lake Chelan.

At Chelan, we bought tickets for a round-trip ride to Stehekin on a big boat named, Lady of the Lake. Stehekin is small village fifty-five miles up the lake, nestled between towering, snowcapped peaks. The view near Stehekin, or anywhere along the upper twenty miles of the lake, is spectacular.

We gave the boat captain instructions to drop us off in a wilderness area fifty miles up the lake, about five miles below Stehekin. My ten-year-old son and I had studied USGS maps to locate a camping spot where there was a crude outhouse and a creek for water.

At our camping spot, the big boat nosed in and slid a ramp to the shore. We slid down the ramp behind our boxes of supplies. Since the boat made the Stehekin run daily, the captain said to signal him with a mirror if we needed to be picked up early. We waved goodbye to the boat and began to set up camp in our beautiful spot surrounded by mountain peaks mirrored with incredible detail in the calm waters of the lake. The mirrored images didn't last long. The wind picked up and soon whitecaps appeared in the lake.

My son and I went to get water. However, we had miscalculated. The creek was a mile away. It looked like we might spend most of our week hauling water from the creek to the camp. But we went on a desperate hunt for another water source. Fifty yards from our camp, I located a big boulder jutting out of the mountain side. From a crack in the rock, clear, cold water flowed, almost like water from an open hydrant. God was good to us, but we weren't out of the water yet, the lake water that is.

We looked for a place flat enough to set up our big tent that all five of us would sleep in. The only suitable spot was on a small point that jutted out into the lake. By the time my wife and I had set up our big tent, the wind was beginning to howl. The tent billowed out like a sail and I feared it might blow away or collapse. So, we tied the tent poles to trees located somewhat upwind.

At this time, I was a practicing Meteorologist, and I realized that the strong marine air push into Western Washington was so deep that the marine air was funneling down through the canyon and could reach 50 or 60 miles-per-hour. We watched the tent until it grew dark. The ominous-looking waves grew to three or four feet high but hadn't hit the tent yet.

When it became too dark to see, we took our chances and crawled into our sleeping bags in the tent, wondering if the lake would rise to claim us during the night. Inside the tent, we heard the wind start that moaning, tornadic noise that tells you it has reached hurricane strength.

Now, waves were breaking on the shore and splattering our tent. No. They were dousing our tent! The tent kept the water out, but certainly not the deafening noise. My wife and I were afraid to go to sleep. If the lake reached us, we needed to be able to get the kids to higher ground before a big wave swept us into the lake.

After two more hours of wind, waves, and splashing water, things seemed to be in a steady state outside. The rest of the family had managed to go to sleep. Since my meteorological experience said conditions probably wouldn't get any worse, I eventually slipped into dreamland.

We survived and awakened to a cloudy, breezy day with the sun winking at us occasionally. We had survived the night and now knew we were up for anything the lake could throw at us. Over the next week, we experienced enough adventure to etch Lake Chelan in our memories for a lifetime.

About the drug cartel in the story—at the turn of the Millennium, the Tijuana Cartel was a large and violent criminal organization. But westward expansion of the Sinaloa Cartel nearly wiped it out. Now, only a remnant exists, but it still pumps heroin, cocaine, meth and marijuana across the border into the U. S. It's not clear who runs the cartel since the demise of its former leaders. Some say it's the leader's sister, others say it's his mother.

For my story, I resurrected the Tijuana Cartel, so I could create some bad guys who have no real-world counterpart to get upset that I used them as villains. I really don't want any strangers with AK-47s knocking on my door.

I hope you liked my main characters, Matt and Randi, and that you enjoyed the story and the dual setting, the Olympic National Park beaches and the Lake Chelan area.

If so, you'll want to read my espionage thriller, *The Janus Journals*, coming soon. It's also set in the Lake Chelan area.

Oh, yes—*No Safe Place* is book one in my Witness Protection series. Expect book two, *No True Justice*, in a couple of months.

H. L. Wegley

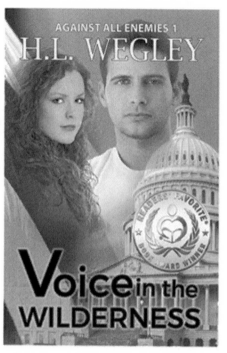

"A terrifyingly real political thriller."

Susan May Warren

Don't miss H. L.Wegley's award-winning, political-thriller series, with romance, *Against All Enemies*:

Book 1: Voice in the Wilderness

Book 2: Voice of Freedom

Book 3: Chasing Freedom (The Prequel)

NO SAFE PLACE